James Clarke

Tears of Things
A Collection of Short Stories

To Beverley
1965-1982
Gonna Make You a Star

Contents

Thou art a soul in bliss; but I am bound
Upon a wheel of fire, that mine own Tears do
Scald like molten lead.
King Lear, IV:7

Tears
of Things

He was sure he wasn't dead. There were the usual signs of consciousness: headache, queasy stomach, gummy eyes. He could hear the maid in the hallway, singing and whistling merrily. He could taste the stale air in the room, a heady mixture of booze and bedclothes and body odour, tinged with hours' old cigarettes. He was lying on the sofa, a foot away from a sliding door. There was an empty wine bottle, some inexpensive glasses, a can of half-drunk Pilsner. A lighted cigarette simmered in an ashtray, and beside the sliding door, near a green papier-mâché piñata of a parrot, hung a series of paintings based on the mystery of the *Mary Celeste*. You could still see the eggs still frying in the pans below deck. You could see the cargo of alcohol untouched. He rubbed his eyes, shook himself, rolled off the sofa, and shuffled into the bathroom to attempt a drink of water. Glancing at himself in the mirror, he looked older, paler, his cheeks and forehead swollen, the sweat on his face cold and his heart pounding slowly and fully in his chest, keeping time with the cracking headache that had ignited behind his eyes. *What,* he asked himself, *am I doing here?*
There was, of course, no answer. At least, no answer which ordinary mortals would accept. But a poet would understand, someone like Virgil. *Optima dies prima*

9

fugit! –the best days are the first to flee! Yes, Virgil, as usual, had the answers. And that, along with seventy-five pence would get you a happy meal at McDonalds. He had to admit, this had all been quite different. There had been no plan, no script, no forethought –just go! The act was spontaneous by any stretch of the imagination. He still couldn't figure out what exactly had happened. He still couldn't understand why he had acted the way he had acted. Maybe he had made a mistake in the way he had acted. Maybe he had gone to extremes, blown things out of proportion, made too much of it. But he *had* to get out of there. He *had* to get away. He was choking up on emotions. He didn't need that shit in his life.

His life up until then had been going reasonably well. At the age of twenty-three, Terence Eagle had just enrolled in a Bachelor of Arts Degree in History at the Kings College of St. John the Baptist and St. Mary Magdalene, a constituent college of the University of London, based in Dorking. Terence had always loved history. Ever since visiting Rome as a child, he had felt an affinity with the past. Walking those sun-nourished streets, the great church bells gonging, was like peering through the barriers of time, like having ones own private link to the ancient world, ones own personal time machine to bygone ages. A strange emotion had filled him in Rome, something more than the narrow cobbled streets and free-standing columns, more than speculation, scholarly argument, discussion, debate –a sense of reality had replaced all those words and pictures in the history books. He felt for the first time like a piece of a story, and being *lived* by that story, a story connected to other stories, connected to art, architecture, culture, civilization –he came to know history.

Being accepted at Kings College of St. John the Baptist and St. Mary Magdalene, was like a dream coming true for Terence. The university ticked all the right boxes for an admirer of the past such as himself. Similar to Rome, there was a sense of antiquity to the place, something embedded in the ivy-covered gables and scarlet creepered walls; the dark gothic arches and pealing clocktowers and long corridors of mahogany doors. Students punted on man-made lakes and picnicked under weeping willows. A giant sculpture of Mary Magdalene –as big as a house and surrounded by angels and archangels –promised eternal bliss in the chapel. Long green quadrangles afforded splendid vistas of the Surrey Hills and freshly-faced students sat poring studiously over great learned books in dusty old libraries.

Founded in 1612, the university traced its origins back to a sixth-century abbey school in the North Downs where the rudiments of academic learning had been taught by Augustine monks and, like many other establishments of the kind, on the destruction of the monasteries, been reorganised by the officers of King Henry VIII and thus acquired its name. It was one of the lesser of the great institutions of higher learning in the UK. It had all the amenities of a prestigious university without any of the superfluous irritations, such as dons, deans, and entry exams. It pandered, in short, to the wannabe Oxbridger, the type who considered themselves part of the intellectual elite, though wanted also to enjoy the lackadaisical atmosphere of any provincial university. Terence had attended the interview at the beginning of the year in the library of the main halls, surrounded by busts of Homer and Socrates and leather-bound volumes scarcely disturbed since the onset of Romanticism. The interview had gone well for him and he had been offered a place on the history degree, which, considering his average 'C' grades, was unexpected. To put it lightly, he was honoured in being accepted at such a place. He thought at most he'd graduate in one of the run-of-the-mill universities that existed up and down the country, gain a Lower Second-Class Honours in some average institution where there were not any great issues, but with a lot of grass and cheap beer and some old lab buildings and half-intelligent students that might produce a genius every twenty years. That'll be the best for him, he thought, what he deserved. Being selected for the Kings College of St. John the Baptist and St. Mary Magdalene was an unexpected surprise, and he felt an awe and delight in going there. The university was like classic ground to him, at least on paper.

The first week at university was mostly admin. There were various intro talks, tours of libraries, computer training sessions, health and safety briefings, familiarisation with timetables and schedules, advisory talks with student reps and directors of study, introductions to Sunday services and personal seminars with the chaplain –the paperwork was endless. On the fourth day he got talking to a second-year undergraduate who said to look out for the Rottweiler in the Classics Department. There was this senior lecturer named Dr. Nicole Barnard who was feared and disliked by most of the students. It was said of her that she came to the task of teaching with a disdain and contempt for those less knowledgeable than herself, as though she perceived between her knowledge and what she could convey lay a gulf so profound that she was unable or even unwilling to close it. Some of her more impartial critics put this down to her loyalty to her subject, describing her as a 'dedicated teacher', one whose dedication blinded her to anything that went on outside the classroom or, at most, outside the halls of the university. Terence met her during the handing out of the term syllabus. She was a woman of advanced middle-age, slightly stuffy and dowdy, her prominent bosom emphasised by highly polished buttons over a floral cardigan which screamed Menopause. She sat very erectly, with all the dignity of the centuries-old college, her posture deliberate and stately, her feet firmly fixed on the ground, almost as though she were trying for the outward part of a religious observation, but not quite reaching it. She read out the term syllabus, pulling long strands of silvery hair out of a military crop and inspecting them between enunciating on Ovid's metamorphoses of ants into humans. Eccentric? But weren't most academics? As long as she wasn't doing dormitory inspections, confiscating personal items, and giving out ten strokes of the cane after class, Terence couldn't give two shits how much of a Rottweiler she was.

They were given their assigned reading for the semester: Augustus' *Res Gestae,* Virgil's *Aeneid*, and the final chapter of E.R. Dodds, *The Greeks and the Irrational.* They were told to read E. R. Dodds for Monday's class, comprise a summary of *Res Gestae* for the same day, and prepare an essay on the *Aeneid* to be submitted the following week. From the Early Modern History syllabus, Terence received another reading list, along with another essay, including a six-hundred-page book on Tudor England to be read for the class on Wednesday. Quite a hefty workload considering it was still Freshers' Week. The honeymoon period had lasted a full three days before the announcement of deadlines and reading assignments. Still, Terence knew it wouldn't be easy. Campus life wasn't all socialising and cheap beer. He would organise himself, set his targets, prioritise and structure, make sure he didn't procrastinate, make sure he kept on top of things. Everything would work itself out –he was sure.

Freshers' Week turned into a blast. Terence met some great new friends in the halls. They got to know each other quickly, going down the student's union and local pubs together. Most nights he and his hallmates gravitated towards a venue on the river, a large barn-like structure that welcomed a mediocre collection of scruffy-haired students wearing beads, beards, and berets, sitting in the alcoves next to the double doors to the kitchen and looking really 'into it,' whatever 'it' was. Terence found the nightspot intriguing, the people fascinating, and the décor inviting, and there were many an evening he found himself sauntering in the dead of night the one-and-a-half-mile trek back to campus; alone and buzzed up on vodka, grunge music, and expresso. One overcast morning he found himself waking in a flatlet off the Dorking high street, the faint sound of traffic out the window and the voices of a TV echoing through the floorboards as he received a soft blowjob. The girl in question was a plain, slightly demure biology student, with cute braids, acne nose, and baby-fat thighs; kept on stressing that she had ne'er done this sorta thing before with exactly the right combination of coyness and a self-depreciation. He had thanked the girl, dried off with some Kleenex tissues, saw himself to the door, and said he'd phone –which he never did.

Between the endless drinking sessions, mindless sex, and induction programmes, Terence tried to get his head down into some work, buying the *Res Gestae,* E.R. Dodds*, and the *Aeneid,* along with the six-hundred pager on Tudor England. In the five-days between studies and classes, he must have read two solid pages of text. His mind was everywhere. He would read and re-read sentences, be distracted, daydream, sometimes finish a whole paragraph without having a clue what he had read or what it was about. It was like part of his brain had dropped away, like a section of his cerebral cortex was experiencing technical difficulties. Maybe he had let the excitement of being away from home for the first time get the better of him. Maybe joining all those societies and clubs wasn't completely necessary. Maybe going out five nights on the trot had killed off a few brain cells. He had to get his act together, and soon. Sure, he could bluff for a while that he had done some of the reading, but not all. As soon as Dr. Barnard started asking him about particular paragraphs or certain dates, he would be floored. There would be no way he could hide his ignorance, she would see it, she was the type. He took himself off to Dr. Barnard's class on Monday morning, filled with tea and wired with caffeine, gnawing on the inside of his cheek like a famished rabbit. He told her he had finished reading the *Res Gestae* and E.R. Dodds (The lie rolled glibly off his tongue), but needed more time on the essay.

'I see,' she said with unconcealed displeasure. 'And why is that?'

'It's the workload,' he explained, 'what with the other classes and it being Freshers' Week.'

Her lips stretched unnaturally thin, and her nostrils curled upwards as if she had just smelt something overly tart. 'I understand you are a mature student?' she asked.

'Yes.'

'Where did you go before you went up?'

'Brooklands College, Weybridge.'

Her nostrils curled ever upwards, 'Oh, yes, the one from the Surrey Access Agency – 'A' level standard, apparently?'

'That's right.'

Her face relaxed, showing a momentary flash of understanding, then stiffened. The voice, hard, sure, authoritarian, said: 'I hope you appreciate that coming to Kings is not like going to any old university. If you wanted that you should have gone to Bristol, or Leeds perhaps. Kings prides itself on its academic rigour. I agree to give you two days extension. I am strictly against such procedures in principle, but in the circumstances, you don't leave me much alternative. Have the essay on my desk on Wednesday morning. Kindly see that this doesn't occur again.'

'Thank you,' said Terence. It came out as a whimper. Terence spent the next two days and nights rubbing his chin and massaging his temples as he tried to cram his brain with facts about Ancient Rome and Tudor England. The essay title for the *Aeneid* was an intellectual feat in itself –*In Auerbach, the analysis and the vindication of realism, as against neoclassical concerns for intellectual precision and rhetorical decorum, reaches its logical perfection. Is this a fair assessment of Auerbach's position? Discuss in regard to the works of Klinger, Büchner, Pöschl, and Otis.* Tuesday, he pulled an all-nighter, burning the midnight oil and scribbling into the grey dawn on the nature and progress of the vocabulary and definition of the word 'soul' in Homeric ideology. He would drift in and out of consciousness, dreaming he was in some shallow grave on the outskirts of Dorking, sharing it with a host of other unfortunate 'D' graders from Dr. Barnard's previous classes. He kept on reminding himself that his predicament was anything but unusual. Most students pulled all-nighters once in a while. You hated yourself for it but didn't change over the course of the three years. Everybody knew the first year didn't count much anyway, it was all to do with the second and final years. The first year was just a preliminary, a settling in before the shit got real and you submitted your dissertation in the last six months. He must confess, it sounded like an excuse to chill out and drink for three whole years with a last-minute panic to hand in your papers, but he wasn't listening to those voices in his head. Anyhow, he had already made some good draft notes on the essay, and that 'kind of' meant he had finished it. He might get a bit nervous in front of Dr. Barnard whilst explaining the situation, but that was to be expected. If the worst came to the worst, if he did turn into a warm piece of piss in front of her, he could always turn nasty, put on the aggravated military style personality, say that he regretted coming to this stuck-up university in the first place to the accompaniment of dark, staring looks. It would be the best for all concerned. But he was sure it wouldn't come to that. He'll pop into her office on Wednesday morning and explain the workload had got on top of him and that he had allowed Freshers' Week to get the better of him. She'd understand. If he can't let her know his problems' she can't help him –right?

He skipped breakfast on Wednesday morning, heading straight over to the Classics Department. He entered the main doors to the department – a drab concrete structure from the late sixties, spoiling an otherwise harmonious baroque campus –and took the lift to the fourth floor. The walk to Dr. Barnard's office seemed long and non-existent, almost like part of him wasn't there, as if he had ceased to exist, as if he had died in that modern monstrosity from the late sixties. Dr. Barnard's door was slightly ajar. He stared at the dark lettering stuck to the opaque bubbled glass with adhesive backing: 111: DR. BARNARD. No one was at the desk. He surreptitiously glanced around at the stacks of books, the windows oil-streaked, cloudy with dust, the bookcases tightly packed with dark, musty-looking volumes.

'Well?'

The voice startled him, a barking voice. Dr. Barnard was standing at the end of one of the bookcases, almost hidden by the imposing structure, as if intending to catch him off guard. He stepped forwards, deeper into the room. Dr. Barnard scowled, her arms folded across her chest, an expression of agonized repugnance wrinkling up her face.

'Well?' she said. 'Do you have it?'

His breath choked in his throat, and he coughed –a glob of phlegm came up. He rolled it around his tonsils, then swallowed. 'No,' he said.

'Why?'

'It's the workload. I've been having problems with it. I was going to ask if I could get another extension. It would really help me out.'

'Another extension!' she said in a tone between bitterness and incredulity. 'I don't see why. All the other students managed to turn their work in on time. Why should I make an exception for *you*?'

'I've been having problems concentrating, what with Freshers' –'

'Freshers' Week is not a legitimate excuse!' she cut him off quickly.

A pause passed between them, infinitesimal in length. She gazed at him. He stared at her. He suddenly felt as if he were wearing too much. His sweater began to itch, his right cheek twitch.

'Frankly none of this looks very good,' she said. 'I've already given you the benefit of the doubt. You seem unable to perform the duties required of this course. I shall like to know why you haven't finished the assignment.'

Terence stood there, his cheek twitching, hands shaking, ears blushing, throat coughing, hunching his neck down into his collar like a turtle drawing into its shell.

'Well …it's.'

Perspiration started pouring down his back. His knees started bending from under him. His nerves felt raw and his eyes felt like they had sunk into his head, pulling the flesh down.

'It's … it's.'

It was like he was disintegrating, being consumed in a chaos of violent emotion, as if he had died a psychological death where the body continued on unawares that the soul had departed.

'It's … it's … *it's* …'

Dr. Barnard continued scowling, her eyes narrowed into two little slits and her lips compressed into a white twist of flesh. 'I don't wish to discuss this anymore,' she said. 'I shall have to have talks with the head of department about you. Do you understand?'

Terence managed a yes.

'Very well, now if you will excuse me.'

He exited the office, his walk hectic, legs bending like rubber, head full of unspoken retorts. He couldn't remember where he went after that. He seemed to walk aimlessly, swiftly, trying to escape the fear that had overtaken him in the office. He couldn't get out of his head how Dr. Barnard had spoken to him. Why had he let her talk to him like that? Why had he allowed the situation to reach such proportions? What was it about her that scared him so? He kept hearing the tone of her voice, the way it had been clipped and precise, uncompromising and forbidding, vibrating with power and command whilst he had stood there shaking like a dog shitting peach seed's. She had *humiliated* him, put him on the cross, torn his ass up one side and down the other. If a hole leading to the underworld had cracked open at that moment in the office, *Christ,* he'd have jumped into it.

After several hours of aimless wandering, he returned to campus. The bright September afternoon had drawn out the students; girls garbed in calf-length dresses and boys in university coloured caps strolled along the tree-shrouded paths which curved through the college grounds. He came to his halls and went up to his room. He drew the curtains, pulled off his clothes, and sank onto the bed. He lay there for an hour, feeling sad, restless, feeling like he had swallowed his own heart – swallowed it whole, without chewing. Maybe he should talk to someone about what had happened, maybe contact the student support service or a union representative, even go up the chain of command to the head of the department. But what was the point in that? He was an insignificant student and Dr. Barnard was a well-respected and published academic. Plus, it would be a little embarrassing to have to explain to someone that he was being bullied by one of the senior lecturers. But he had to do something. He'd be damned if he was going to sit back and take the scoldings of some frigid old spinster. The most important thing to do was not let it get to him, remind himself he had achieved a lot already by coming to the university; that he was a capable and intelligent student with the potential to achieve a decent qualification of a degree. Everything would sort itself out –he was sure.

He sat up and positioned himself towards the TV, switching it on. An oft rerun of the eighties series, *The Love Boat* was showing. A group of aging safecrackers were attempting to rob half a million in loot from the cruise ships' vault. He stared at the bumbling burglars, gazing gormless as he chewed his nails and tried to remember the names of the actors who were appearing. There was some guy– 'fingers' –who had been in the *Cocoon* films, and a distinguished looking actor he remembered from some sci-fi programme when he was a kid. Maybe he was seeing everything that had happened in the office wrongly. Maybe it was mostly his fault. Yes, she had had come down hard on him but he was partially responsible for that. Not to put too fine a point on it, he had fucked up by not doing the work. Sure, the whole incident had been embarrassing, but worse than that was the guilt –the guilt at over-indulging in the joys and distractions of Freshers' Week, the guilt at having not lived up to the standards he had expected of himself. Maybe he just wasn't cut out for higher education, maybe he'd bitten off more than he could chew, taken on more than he could handle, wasn't of the right calibre for the prestigious Kings College of St. John the Baptist and St. Mary Magdalene. Maybe Dr. Barnard had done him a favour in speaking to him like that, given him a few home truths, helped knock down a few walls he had built up about university life and what it was like; cosy images of cricket greens, antique libraries, and dreaming spires. He should be condoning the woman not condemning her. The canned laughter from the TV spilled across the room. He could hear indistinct chatter in the communal kitchen. He hit the power button on the remote, shut off the TV, made himself a cup of tea, did some reading till late afternoon, and went to bed.

21

He got up early next morning, managing to anticipate his alarm by an hour. He packed a minimum of clothes, the basic toiletries, a Walkman, cassette player, some headphones, his newly purchased copy of Virgil's *Aeneid*. He could feel the butterflies in his stomach as he left the room, making as little noise as possible as he made his way down the hallway, listening to the slumbered breathing of his housemates as he took the stairs to the ground floor. The air outside was cool. The morning song-birds were twittering and a slow careless breeze rustled the trees. Under a lighting sky, the gabled roofs of the university took on an added brightness from a tracery of sparkling frost which still clung to them. It was the beginning of autumn. Soon the days would wane and the trees would don their vibrant hues and a low, pervading wind would sweep over the college grounds. Students would go home for the lapse of the festive season and return in the new year to start the long, arduous preparation for exams. He picked up his bag, slung it over his shoulder and stepped into the morning. The smile on his face as he closed the door was a small one, almost not there. But it was a smile.

His great-grandfather had loved Acker Bilk, particularly his piece *Stranger on the Shore,* from the single of the same name. He had had the song on vinyl record and would whenever the occasional demanded play to it on his small turntable. He could still see his great-grandfather pulling the record out of its sleeve, blowing gently on the surface, kneeling down next to the deck, placing the record on the record-player and, with complete precision, putting the needle on the track.

His long, gnarled fingers would twist the volume too high and he would arch his neck, his face filled with emotion as the tender sounds of a clarinet issued from the speakers. What a soft, kind song it was, just like his great-grandfather, such a wonderful piece, such a weirdly sad and happy melody. It was strange to how it could be both. But it was so.

Terence clamped the collar of his coat around his throat, hugging himself against the cold as he sat in the waiting room at Calais. How odd, he thought, that *Stranger on the Shore* would be playing now, the clarinet sounds pouring from the loudspeakers over the stone-topped tables and black wooden chairs, trying in its own vain bid to instil warmth in the waiting room. The waiting room reminded him of a public lavatory. It had all the hallmark features: gleaming tiled walls; discoloured floors, uninviting grey doors, palely lit by rows of naked yellow bulbs which gave the impression of curried moonlight. People sat around on their own, a scattered, grubby, tired lot, withdrawn and sulky, huddled against the cold, no one talking to each other, nobody admitting to curiosity or fellow feeling, their faces vulnerable and introspective.

Terence drew his eyes up and stared at the large-faced clock suspended over the ticket office. Still another two hours before his train to Rome. For a moment he had a lapse of purpose. He nearly got up and headed out the door, but then reminded himself why he was leaving and resumed his course of action. It was like there was a strange ambivalence inside of him, a gathering of contrary elements, like being caught between two opposing worlds. He felt lost and confused, but at the same time happy and certain, like a ball on a tangled yarn, the parts that were untangled were available, useable; the rest was a mess, useless until it was untied. Whether it would ever be untied he didn't know.

The train for Rome left on schedule, prompt at quarter past midnight. He boarded one of the carriages and found an empty compartment, curled up on the seat and watched through half-closed lids as the train moved into the night. He changed trains at Paris, taking a sleeper to Milan via Geneva. He was exhausted by the time he reached Milan. He should have arrived five hours earlier but had taken the wrong train at Geneva and found himself in Bern before he realised it. In Bern, he had wasted another three hours in confusion before finally boarding the right train and travelling non-stop, arriving in Milan at half past two in the afternoon and Rome a few hours after that. In Rome, he took himself to the information desk, booked a hotel, bought a map, and headed into the streets. Thankfully the hotel wasn't far from the Termini, just a few minutes' walk. He made his way around the back of a church, walked down some steps and entered a narrow alley crowded with potted plants and scooters. A solid, grey building stood halfway down the alley, a tall, battered tenement block with large windows covered in prison-like grilles. A small brass plaque was fixed to the door.

Hotel Paradiso –third floor, it read.

He pressed the intercom, and was buzzed through the door. He passed into a cool hallway. To the left of the hallway was a precipitous marble staircase with a turn-of-the-century birdcage elevator beside it. The elevator creaked and hummed to life as he called it. He alighted the elevator on the third landing and walked into a dimly-lit foyer. The concierge resembled a human offspring of the building, all two-hundred-odd pounds of him crammed into a five-foot-five body, with small dark eyes almost hidden behind an enormous face.

Terence signed the register, took his key, and walked up a floor to his room. His room was a pleasant surprise. It was eloquently furnished, spacious and high-ceilinged, with a large hanging fan and oriental carpet. There was a mahogany closet, a walnut desk, a reclining balcony with a rail of oak. A clown with purple dreadlocks sat on an ornately carved chest-of-draws, and on the walls, near the entrance, hung large tapestries –images of cherubs, titans, sportive nymphs and satyrs, some rustic work with a group of marine deities; Hannibal crossing the Alps. The most impressive tapestry showed a bull and lion locked in a death struggle; the lions teeth sunk into the hind of the bull, its mane dark with blood. Terence crossed to the balcony, pulled back the shutters, and gazed out at a well cultivated garden. Behind and above the garden could be seen irregular masses of buildings climbing the slopes of the Quirinale Hill. And the whole was dominated by a slender white villa that blossomed out at the top, similar to the manner of a baroque villa, into overhanging designs. He stood there in silence, leaning his elbows on the balustrade, sighing, drawing a kind of sustenance from the scene, a perfect antidote to his recent wayworn mood. Unfortunately, he had no time to soak in this delightful pageant. There was something he needed to do, something he had promised himself he must see when first arriving in Rome.

He made his way back onto the streets, taking the road to the Termini and hailing a taxi outside the main entrance. The taxi swept into the flow of traffic, moving down one of the thoroughfares, joining the endless vehicles towards the Colosseum. The avenues were crowded that time of the day, and the traffic jammed at the fountains and in the side-streets. The taxi driver made slow progress, breaking, swearing, hitting the roof of the vehicle and taking shortcuts down alleys; passing churches and gardens, swerving around clusters of nuns, barely escaping collision with an old man dragging a fruit cart and coming to a stop outside a pair of wrought-iron gates.

'This is *it!*' said the taxi driver.

Terence checked his watch, five past four. He still had enough time for a slight detour. There was another place he wanted to see not far away, a place he knew his great-grandfather would be proud of him visiting. He paid the taxi driver and crossed the street, making his way to the end of the road and entering through another set of gates. Pleasantly planted lawns greeted him as he entered the gates. There was a long trim gravel pathway and, to the left, shaded amongst umbrella-shaped pines, rows of headstones. The headstones were simple and unadorned, rectangular pieces of granite laid out in parallel columns, each one polished and exactly the same as the other, except the names they bore. He walked along, staring at the headstones, reading the names, most of them of young men –those that had given their lives in the last war. His eyes fell on a grave with no name.

A SOLDIER
OF THE
1939-1945
WAR
✝
KNOWN ONTO GOD

He sniffed and stared at the headstone, stood there for a moment, knelt and cleared away some cobwebs at the base. The muscles of his chin trembled, and his throat shuddered.

'It's not right!' he said. 'It's just *not* right.'

His watch said four-twenty. He rose to his feet, brushed himself off, bowed at the headstone, and walked back to the gates and out the cemetery.

'What do you mean, you're closing!'

'Four-thirty close.'

'But I was told you close at five.'

'Not five, four-thirty.'

'But I was told five.'

'Five o'clock close, last entry, four-thirty.'

'Just ten minutes,' Terence implored. 'It's important to me.'

'I am very sorry, sir,' said the young Italian man, fishing out a cigarette and lighting it.

Terence looked at him with pleading eyes, trying to give his most suppliant expression.

'Okay,' the young man mumbled, detaching the cigarette from his lips and tracing smoke from each nostril. 'I give you five minutes.'

Terence entered the wrought-iron gates into a dense collection of headstones. Serried rows of tombs, half-hidden by blossoming wisteria, rose up a terraced slope to a gleaming white pyramid. Dark cypresses and pines stood close by to the pyramid, silhouetted against it and forming dark groves around the tombs. Terence made his way along a path, stepping carefully over roots that knotted the way. He followed a bend, went through a stone archway, crossed through a patch of sunlight, passed through another archway. To his right was an open part of the cemetery. Sun-bleached funerary and cinerary lay scattered across a lawn. There was a wheelbarrow and a cluster of old women in black brushing up leaves and pulling ivy away from tombs. Beyond them other old women in black were raking the leaves into neat little piles amongst the trees. A stone chapel stood in the corner; a marble catafalque standing nearby –with stained laurels in the windows, and some other old women in black were washing the red-and-white floor. On the other side of the lawn, near some columns, looking conspicuously alone – stood a small brown headstone. Terence walked over to the headstone and read the inscription:

This Grave
Contains all that was Mortal,
Of a

Young English Poet
Who
On his Death Bed,
In the Bitterness of his Heart
At the Malicious power of his Enemies,
Desired
These Words to be engraved on his Tomb Stone
Here lies one whose Name was writ in Water
February 24th 1821

Terence sank onto a nearby bench, pulled out a cigarette, lit it, and stared at the headstone. The crickets were going crazy around him, whipping themselves up into frenzies, rubbing their little leathery thighs together and chirring in unison, as if singing a lullaby to the dead. He took a drag from the cigarette and flicked the ash over a bouquet of variegated flowers. It was hard to believe. Just below him, no more than six feet, were bones, heaps of bones, bones upon bones going back centuries upon centuries. He imagined tree roots growing out of shattered rib-cages, tendrils protruding from fleshless mouths, skulls and skeletons meshed together in an endless display of decline. He imagined eyes disintegrating in sockets, skin peeling from bone, carcases crawling with worms, things rotting, things blackening.

Turning to dust.

To earth.

To nothing.

'It's *not* right!' he said, choking out the words and turning away from the young poet's grave. It was so final, so unequivocal. Life was fleeting, ephemeral, a brief interruption in time, an interval between love and pain, and after that –dust, ashes. Did all this mean that the soul wasn't eternal? Maybe it meant that the soul was not eternal –*yet*. He couldn't tell. All he knew was that he was afraid, afraid of not knowing what was beyond this life, afraid of not knowing whether there was something or nothing.

Unable to console himself, he rose from the bench, gathered his belongings, shot his cigarette into the grass, and made for the exit. As he neared the gates something stopped him in his tracks. Lifting his eyes, he saw the most amazing sight –starlings, thousands of rose-coloured starlings. They swooped and swirled, twisting and turning, moving like clouds through the purple sky. He watched as they flitted and dived, flying with a shrill cleaving of their wings over the dark graves and darker belt of trees. They flew downwards, moving as one body and nestling amidst the trees. There they sat, singing their cheerful songs –twitter-twitter, chirp-chirp, chirr-chirr, like a choir of small eager voices in darkened boughs, countless earnest prayers amongst tangled limbs. Even the chorus of crickets couldn't compete with their noise. There was something mysterious to the birdsong, a quality that was at once familiar and strange, alien yet native, intrinsically woven into the fabric of the cemetery, yet somehow transcending it. The trees seemed fixed, frozen in time, the birdsong flowing through the leaves, pouring down through the branches and into the earth, mingling with the bones and dust and long-lost ages.

□

He was awake. In fact, he had been awake for an hour, lying on top of the bed and staring around the room, giving himself time to shed the sleep from his mind, to allow the visions of the night to give way to the day. He had fallen into a deep sleep after leaving the cemetery, sleeping heavy and waking early, feeling fatigued and disorientated, not used to the long-haul journeys across continents. He swung his legs out of bed and went into the bathroom. Glancing at himself in the mirror, he looked younger, less anxious, his eyes wide and lips curved in youthful expectancy. Gone were the usual spinal aches and pains he had become accustomed to during those first few damp moments of the morning; gone the world-weary look. He went back into the bedroom, crossed over to the window and opened the shutters. Light flooded into the bedroom, filling every corner and niche, wrapping everything in beams of sunlight. The clown on the chest-of-draws smiled more broadly than ever. The bull and lion in the tapestry looked like they were romping rather than fighting. He put his head out the window and looked down at the garden. A gentle mist rose from the flowers, evidence of rain during the night, and some scattered white clouds cruised the sky. He had been wakened by the sound of a gardeners' hose pricking the tough rosebush leaves and, looking out the shutters, he could see a toothless dotard sweeping the flagstones. He left the window, went into the bathroom, showered, towered, dressed, gathered his possessions, picked up his guidebook, map, sunglasses et al, and left the hotel. It was a clear morning in Rome. Breakfasters drank coffee standing outside cafes. Market workers unpacked boxes of vegetables and fruit. Tourists disembarked from coaches, blabbering in their various languages. He spent some time in a souvenir gift shop near the Termini, then passed down the *Via Cavour*, taking one of the streets leading to the exhibition hall and making his way down towards the Forum. The site of splendid buildings lay everywhere, strange but seriously wonderful places with walls of burnt sienna and red, the weathered stucco surfaces emblazoned with posters of opera singers and underground artists, the occasional monument appearing between the buildings, half-eaten structures, large ornate edifices still standing despite the ravages of the centuries.

Around noon he found a park and rested till the end of siesta, then wandered some more, finding a restaurant beside the Tiber and spending the remainder of the day at the Colosseum. He started making his way back to the hotel around five. He decided on a quick drink in a bar before going back, some small unassuming place tucked away in one of the narrow roads near the Pantheon. It was a tiny sweatbox of a place, no more than a storage closet, with redbrick walls, crappy mirror ball, and a thin chrome pole in the middle of the floor which seemed to support the building. There were many feet, and beyond these, alongside the walls, trampling voices yelled. Shadowed figures whirled about, vying for space, colliding, spilling their drinks and hollering, whilst in the corner, on a small raised platform, a transvestite in a clinging gown stood in a white-blond wig, a sort of Latin Dietrich, attempting a rendition of Gloria Gaynor's *I am What I am*, making up in volume for whatever she lost in quality.

Terence did a breast stroke through the numerous combinations of bumping flesh, elbowing his way through the people. The place was busy for that time of the evening. He couldn't figure if the people were starting early or finishing late, had come from work and were on their way home or where at work and had paused for a shot or two. It didn't matter. He didn't want to become a love customer in the place, and he wasn't. He turned his attention to the bar, noticing a girl sitting on the last stool, against the wall. She looked desultory, sad looking, her head down, reading a dog-eared, folded-over, obviously cheap paperback with such slow concentration that her lips were discernibly forming the words. There was something about her, he thought, something about her simple black dress and small white features –the scent of vulnerability, of over-sensitivity, she wore it the way other women wear perfume. He stiffened, took a breath, and skirted across the dance floor towards her, giving his very best grin.

'What are you reading?' he asked her.

She held up the book cover. The title said: '*Twilight of the Sexes. The Chequered Career of a Madison Avenue Account Executive.*'

'Sounds interesting,' he lied. 'Maybe I can borrow it sometime.'

She managed a faint, humourless smile.

'You look English?' he said, searching for some pretext to prolong the conversation.

'Australian.'

'You look a bit Eurasian as well.'

32

'That's because I'm half Chinese.'

'So, why are you in Rome?'

'I'm a student here.'

'A student, huh, what are you studying?'

'Music.'

'Any particular style?'

'Glam Rock.'

'Really, who's your favourite Glam Rock artist?'

'Bowie.'

'Of course; did you know that Bowie's first appearance was on *Top of the Pops*? You may have heard of it, the British chart show.'

'I know.'

'He was wearing this all-sparkling body suit and singing *Starman*. One of his best performances by all accounts.'

'Yeah, I know.'

'So, what's your favourite Bowie song?'

'Heroes'

'Sure, his 'Berlin' period. Did you know that the song was originally conceived as an instrumental?'

'Yeah.'

'Personally, I was more into R&B myself: Marvin Gaye, Stevie Wonder, Aretha Franklin, that sort of thing; well, my parents were which kinda made me.'

She looked away, staring idle into the middle distance, like a seer in a trance. His friendly overture wasn't going well. Terence pursed his lips, and looked around. The Latin Dietrich had disappeared and been replaced with a four-to-six chorus line of grizzled old men in outrageous female drag. They linked arms and were kicking high as they sang *Happy Days Are Here Again*. Pausing then, and concentrating so as not to make a balls of it, Terence said: 'This is a pretty interesting place.'

'If you say.'

'Yes, I think it is … do you mind if I tell you something?'

'G' ahead.'

'Forgive me if I'm being personal, but you look like a girl that's been burned recently.'

'Scolded. Repeatably.'

'Well, us men aren't all monsters you know.'

'Men are overgrown schoolboys, always were.'

'Hey, at least we don't have to go to the bathroom without a support group.'

She gave off one of those laughs people make to show they appreciate the effort someone made to make a joke –'Hhmmheeeemm!'

Terence ordered the drinks, for him a gin-and-tonic and for her a Martini dry. She told him her name was Mandii (Mandii with two i's not a 'y'), and that her father was some big shot property developer from Perth who owned several places around the world, one of which she was staying in whilst living in Rome. After flunking out of college in her teens, she had drifted for several years, living at home and doing temporary work; helping around the house and riding around the streets with her contemporaries smoking pot. In her twenties she had gone back to college, applying to the University of New South Wales and being accepted on a Contemporary Music Degree. There had been a few complications in her first year and she had been granted leave due to her suffering from some mental disorder, the diagnoses coming back from the doctors that she had social phobia. Her parents had placed her with a local therapist who specialised in helping people master new approaches to dealing with out-dated belief systems they held about themselves, particularly the feelings they got around intimate encounters. She had

34

been burnt several times in love –scolded repeatedly, and as a result had developed an acute form of 'dating anxiety.' Before coming to Rome, she had been learning with the aid of the therapist how not to fall victim to the social problems and negative self-judgements that had been assailing her. She went on to say that the times when her social phobia did rear its ugly head, which it made it difficult for her to focus on her studies, she would take herself off to some bar and sit on her own. This didn't seem to bother her, and in fact excited her. She liked to sit surrounded by noisy, happy people. She enjoyed melting away into the crowds, drinking alone, but not entirely ignored, to immerse herself, as she said, in the perception of, without the participation in, the business of other people. There was some charged excitement for her of going into a bar on her own, somewhere where no one knew her name and no one seemed to care, a gratitude to drink anonymously, a desire to sit undisturbed, unmolested by life. Terence explained to her his own situation at university, and how things were happening nevertheless. Without getting too specific, he implied that his degree was extremely demanding and important and that he was in Rome taking a *hiatus* to clear his mind, like a sabbatical, whilst getting a little inspiration for an essay he was writing on Virgil.

They spent a few hours together, talking about this and that, hitting it on and off, smoking cigarettes and drinking dark liquors. They left the bar around three a.m., spilling out with the rest of the partygoers into the morning streets and taxiing back to her apartment. Her place was located on a housing estate in the periphery of Rome, one of those high-rise apartment blocks from after the war, modish and skinny and unpainted, looking like a concept from the mind of a neorealist filmmaker. The apartment was charming, not elegant, but comfortable. There were some items that looked like oriental imports, some old pottery, an overstuffed lounge chair, a built-in bar. A giant green papier-mâché piñata of a parrot stood on a corner shelf and a series of paintings hung on the walls, based on what Terence guessed was the *Mary Celeste.*

'Want a drink?' Mandii asked, unclasping a ribbon bow hair-clip from the side of her head. 'Gin on the rocks?'

'Sound's great,' replied Terence.

She tossed the hair-clip onto the table, walked over to the drinks cabinet, took out a bottle of Gordon's Dry, and headed into the kitchen. She opened the refrigerator and pulled out a tray of ice, banged the door shut with her foot, and proceeded to break the ice up with a bread knife. Terence walked over to a sliding door which lead to a narrow balcony, looking out at the night.

'I like your apartment,' he said.

'Yeah? I'm glad.'

'I like it here. You're lucky to have such a generous father.'

'He has his uses.'

'I love this city you know –Rome.'

'Oh?'

'I used to come here as a kid. It must be my favourite place on earth.'

'Is that why you're running away here.'

Terence felt the shock register on his face before he could hide it. 'What makes you say that?' he asked.

'Isn't that why most people travel alone, because they're trying to escape something?'

'I *told* you, I'm writing an essay. I've been given time off university – like a sabbatical.'

She smiled slightly. 'I see. One piece of ice or two?'

'One,' said Terence, trying to recover his equilibrium. She plopped one piece of ice into his glass, two in hers, and walked over to him.

'Here we go,' she said, handing him his glass. They both tasted their drinks and stood in silence. She seemed to be watching him intently, gazing at him like a cat from behind her glass. She went on: 'So, you're a fan of Rome you say.'

'Yes, I like the heaviness of it here.'

'The heaviness?'

'Yes, every time I've come to Rome, especially Rome, I feel a heaviness.'

'Never heard Rome described like that before.'

'It's like a weight, a pressure –a *heaviness*. Well, it's more an energy if I'm quite honest. It's like I can feel the layers of the ages here, like I can sense all the people that have lived and worked here; like a rock-strata going back through the centuries. I visited this place yesterday, the Protestant Cemetery, have you heard of it?'

'No.'

'It must be the most beautiful place I've ever seen. You know for a moment I thought I heard the dead speak to me through these birds. It was like the souls of dead people were animating them, living *through* them –I've never felt so much joy in my life.'

Mandii stared at him with a nebulous look, abstractly rubbing the edge of her glass against the side of her neck. 'Want a refill?' she said.

'Sure.'

She went and got the drinks.

'You're a deep one,' she said as she poured the drinks. 'Personally, I never went in for psycho-spiritual explanations of life, not even with my psychiatrist, something to do with my Catholic upbringing, not that I believe in God or anything, most Catholics don't. The truth is I'm weary of philosophical conundrums. I've heard one too many. So, I tend to not meet an idea like that head on.'

'You're Catholic?'

'Educated at a mission school in Macau.'

'I thought you said you were from Perth?'

'I was –am, but we moved around a lot with my pops business.' She dropped more ice into their glasses and walked back over.

'Well, here's to the everlasting city,' she said, raising her glass and tossing her drink back in one swallow. Terence swallowed his own drink and gave off a tenuous smile. She turned and walked to a drawer in the kitchen, opened it and drew out a small plastic container. She emptied the contents of the container onto the counter and, with a credit card, began to divide three neat little lines on the counter.

'Want some blow?' she asked.

'No thanks,' said Terence.

She withdrew from her purse a bank note, and proceeded to roll it into a cylinder.

'Last chance'

'No thanks.'

Wearing a smile, she brought a line up to her face and snorted. After loading each nostril, she stood upright, swayed a little, and performed a small pirouette in the kitchen, her hair tossing back and forth across her face. Terence took several swallows of his drink, set it down, and walked over to her. She slipped her hand between his thighs, reaching down and squeezing him between her palms. He started working the buttons of her shirt undone, exploring the free surfaces of the skin underneath, the curves of collar bone and breast. She threw back her neck, her limbs shuddering, eyes

38

staring. He kissed her fast and furious. She responded with her own enthusiasm, thrusting her tongue into his mouth and grabbing his love handles. They heaved, fondled, moved positions, lurched, strained, grabbed, connected, and then –*Voilà l'amour!*

Afterwards they lay on the carpet, in front of the sliding door, in each other's arms, two exhausted bodies in an empty space, lying there, silent, naked.

'You don't want to get involved with me,' said Mandii.

'Why?'

'You don't know me. I'm not some paragon of virtue.'

'I know, I know. Your day job is just that –*day job*, but by night you entertain you're alter-ego. Am I right?'

'I haven't been straight with you.'

Terence gave her a wry smile, 'But I like your name.'

She detached herself from him, slid away and got to her feet. She walked into the kitchen and poured herself another drink. She plopped the ice in the glass and went over to the sliding door, arms crossed, looking across the apartment blocks. He sensed a terrible tension in her, something she was keeping deep within only with the greatest effort, something he could not hope to reach, not even knowing what it was. He only knew the moment they had shared so strongly moments before was, now, completely dissipated.

'So, what's this this about?' Terence asked, slightly nervous. 'What are you trying to tell me?'

'I thought you knew.'

'Knew what?'

'That I'm a prostitute.'

He stared at her, unable to speak, trying to remember to breathe. She continued to stare out the window at the apartments, gazing with those dark sullen eyes at nothing. He waited, silent. Then, at last, broke the silence, saying: 'That's some announcement.'

'I thought you knew.'

'No.'

'I'm sorry.'

'So, how does this work?'

'What do you mean?'

'I mean, how do we do this? Will I wake up tomorrow with a bill?'

'I invited you here because I *wanted* to!' Her eyes narrowed. She raised her glass and swirled the chunk of ice around, irritatedly. Terence's stomach tightened.

'And what about the other stuff?' he said.

'What other stuff?'

'The stuff about your father being some big shot property developer; about you reading music, about you being the poor little rich girl; that was all just James Bond time?'

She stood a second, motionless, without speech; then shook herself as though out of sleep, saying: 'Have you ever wished you were somebody else? Have you ever fantasized about waking up and finding that your life was a dream, that you were somebody completely different, and that you could start all over again?'

'Yes, I have.'

'Well, that's how I live my life. I go about pretending I'm somebody else, pretending that my life is different to what it is, just like Suzie Wong in that old film. I'm the girl who rides on the Star Ferry saying I'm Mee Ling, nice rich girl whose father owns many houses and more cars than you can count, when really I'm just a dirty little yum-yum girl who hangs around bars trying to get men to take her back to their hotels.'

'So how did it happen,' Terence asked. 'How did you become a prostitute?'

She poured herself another drink and looked at it before she drank it. Then she looked at Terence and said:

40

'How does anyone become a prostitute. I used to waitress for a while in Perth, first at a restaurant in the business district, then at a late-night hangout in the suburbs, where most of the waitresses hooked on the side. I was introduced to a man there who ran an agency that set girls up on very Class A dates –the theatre, dinner at some top-end restaurant, and then a couple of hours sex in a midtown hotel. I ended up zeroing in on one of my customers, some property developer who said I could use his apartment in Rome whenever I wanted.'

Terence swallowed hard. 'And you're … you're Australian?'

'Born and raised. My mother came from the inland province of Fujian. She took herself like many girls do, to Hong Kong to make money. She met my father there one night and they fell in love. He was a young American guy on R&R from Vietnam. They spent just five days together before he returned to the war. He sent her a letter two weeks later, telling her he'd gotten wounded and was being sent to Japan. She never heard from him again. We lived in Macau for a while after that. I was placed in a missionary school whilst my mom worked as a launderer for the mission. In the early eighties we moved back to Hong Kong and my mom started working the streets again. She ended up meeting another guy there, an Australian soldier, a sweeter, older man, shy and lonely. He married her and took us both back to his farm in Queensland. Unfortunately, things didn't quite work out on the farm. My Australian stepfather tried to rape me on my thirteenth birthday, and so my mother and me left him and moved to Perth. The rest as you say is history.'

There was a pause. Their eyes held each other's, and for a moment Mandii's face was expressionless. Terence

41

stared at her, dumbfounded. He didn't know how to react. He felt distant –as though he was looking at her under glass.

'I'm sorry Mandii,' he said, 'if that's your name.'

'It is.'

She smiled feebly, knocked back the dregs of her drink, and walked over to the stereo.

Watching her search through the records in the rack, Terence said: 'Maybe you can do something else … you're still young … you're not meant for this sort of thing … isn't there something else you'd rather do, tell me?'

Her smile indicated his naïve question. 'You think I do this because I like it? I do it because I earn more money than I could elsewhere. I have a lot of responsibilities. It doesn't matter what I do. I know what you're thinking about me, but you're *wrong!* Everybody treats me like a queen.'

Terence looked down at his nakedness, 'So how does it work?' he asked, 'with your clients?'

'I get them to buy me drinks, very much like what you were doing tonight. Most of them are businessmen in town for a convention, just looking for fun, want to take me out to dinner and fuck me in the space of an hour, easy work.

'What about your sugar daddy, the guy who owns this place?'

'I see him one week out of four, whenever he happens to be free from business trips or commitments to his wife. I pick him up at the airport and he whisks me away to somewhere like Venice or Milan, buys me pretties; ruby slippers, silk kimonos, jewels, allocates me the occasional gram of coke. Italy *molto* expensive you know!'

She smiled again –but with a satisfied self-confidence that he found disconcerting. She switched on the stereo, selected a record from the rack and inserted it on the player. A song filtered out of the speakers. The strains of a violin filled the air, along with the strumming of guitars and the rhythmic beat of drums –*Heroes,* by David Bowie.

Her face softened to the music, the veins beneath her temples seen clearly through the pallid skin. For a moment they didn't know anything, the both of them engrossed in the music and staring at the other. They slid down together on the sofa, and she fitted her body against his. The first suggestion of dawn could be seen out the sliding doors, paling the sky. They stared at it, their breathes' heavy, arms draped over each other. Slowly, over the distance of twenty minutes the sky softened to a timid blue and the clouds were blushed like a ripe mango. Lights still winked in a thousand buildings, as if they were not yet sure of the sun.

Terence leaned over and planted a kiss on Mandii's cheek. 'You're not a dirty yum-yum girl,' he said. 'Sure,' she mumbled.

He wrapped his arms around her and stared out at the dawn-streaked city, staring at those flickering lights as his eyes stung with tears. He couldn't remember falling asleep.

☐

He was sure he wasn't dead. There were the usual signs of consciousness: headache, queasy stomach, gummy eyes. He could hear a maid in the hallway, singing and whistling merrily. He could taste the stale air in the room, a heady mixture of booze and bedclothes and body odour, tinged with hours' old cigarettes. He rose to his elbows, eased himself from the sofa, and headed into the bathroom. He twisted the right-hand faucet on the sink, letting a cold jet of water spill into his hands. As he leant forward, he checked himself out in the mirror. The news wasn't good. A mass of swollen meat stared back at him. Above the meat hung a crown of derelict hair, lying in matted, crinkled patterns across his forehead. He filled the basin and splashed his face, took out his penis, and relieved his burdened bladder into the bowl. He finished peeing, scowled at his reflection, wiped the detritus fluids from his penis, and proceeded back to the living room. Before arriving, he turned into the bedroom near the door. The room reminded him of a teenagers' pad. The dressing table was covered in knick-knacks; combs, brushes, magazines, hair extensions. Photos of rock stars were tacked over the makeup mirror. Garish paperbacks were stacked against the wall. He noticed a business card on the dressing table, the lettering on the card printed in florid script, like a wedding invitation.

Mandii

Offering a unique and unhurried service
For the discerning gentleman
In and out calls

Coming out of the bedroom, he entered the hallway and went back into the living room. Mandii was dressed and sitting upright on the sofa, feet and knees together, leaning forward and dipping into a line of coke on the coffee table.

'What are you doing?' asked Terence.

'Dingo's breakfast,' replied Mandii.

'You should be drinking coffee!'

44

She made a sort of laugh, like a hollow mocking sound, as if seething at the absurdity of his comment.

'Look,' he said. 'I don't give a shit what you do. I'm only saying you should be a little careful with that stuff.'

'Thanks,' she said, 'thanks for the lesson, dad.'

He groaned, twisting his mouth in irritation, watching as she filled her nostrils with the gleaming white powder.

'So, what are you doing today?' he asked, trying to make his voice sound normal.

'Well,' she said, wiping her nose, answering matter-of-factly, 'I'm going to have a bath, paint my toenails, visit the spa, and then go shopping.'

'I suppose you'll be working later?'

'I suppose.'

'I suppose you'll be fixing a few lines of coke with it as well?'

'I suppose.'

She bent down to take another hit, shifting nostrils and sucking on the bank note as if it were oxygen.

'You know,' Terence said, 'I feel sorry for you Mandii. I thought there was a nice girl somewhere under all that neurosis and powder habits. Obviously, I was mistaken.'

Mandii cast a fast glance at him, as if mystified by his comment. The cocaine clung to her lips and lashes and patched across her face, making her look like a demented clown. 'What's yer trouble, *mate*?' she said in a pronounced New South Wales accent.

'What?'

'Whose eyes do you think you're trying to pull the wool over?'

'What're you talking about?'

'I'm talking you and your monopoly on truth. You come here blowing the roof off, spouting some pretentious crap about finding yourself in Rome; about how everything's deep and meaningful here all because you visited a few cemeteries. You've given me all this bunkum when you don't believe a word of it yourself!'

'Who said I don't believe a word of it!'

She looked at Terence with amused contempt. 'Oh, that's rich, you're something else! Go back to your hotel, sweetie. Go take a long look at yourself in the mirror.'

'I did that already.'

'Yeah, and what did you see?'

'I saw a man that was searching for something more than what was in the history books. I saw the things that he valued most had no intrinsic value in themselves. I saw that everything in the world is as it should be, and that there's nothing certain in life except that we must one day lose it.'

She made a scoffing sound. 'Oh, you're priceless! It must take a lot of effort to convince yourself your shit doesn't stink, especially when your heads lost in the clouds.'

'I'm not sure I like the way you're seeing me.'

'Oh, and what about the way you're seeing *me*–just a fuck!'

'What?'

'Well, that's right. That's how you saw me at the bar. A quick bash, an easy lay, a piece of fun while taking a cultured break on the continent.'

Terence looked at her questioningly. 'I'm leaving,' he said.

'Okeydoke.'

'It was nice meeting you.'

'Byebye now.'

46

He pulled on his clothes, tying up his shoelaces quickly and zipping up his flies, his eyes hardly meeting hers as she tapped out another breakfast line on the coffee table.

'I hope you enjoy your shopping,' he said as he gathered his coat from the arm of a chair and made for the door.

'Oh, I forgot to say,' she said as he approached the door. 'I thought you oughta' know. There's something else about me, something I didn't mention last night.'

'Oh, what's it this time,' said Terence, looking at her over his shoulder and clenching his jaw, 'you're not going to tell me you're from the moon, are you.'

'No,' she replied. 'My names not Mandii – it's Joseph.' Terence paused, his mouth open, his body unmoving, trying to register what she had just said. Outside the window, thick rolling clouds descended, casting blue shadows across the apartment blocks.

How long he walked he couldn't remember. He moved with his head bent low, hands stuffed in his pockets, passing from one street to the next, from one cobbled passage to the next, from one piazza to the other. It was Sunday and the traffic was light in Rome. Clouds doubled up on each other. Thick swoons of mist hung over the buildings. The whole of Rome seemed one colour, solid grey, a dull reflection of the uniform sky. Terence got on the Metro and got off somewhere and started walking west, moving between the cool shadows of tall buildings, past long rows of brownstone houses, down dark streets into darker crooked alleys. He was jogging when he turned onto the *Via di San Gregorio,* angling off at the Colosseum and plunging into the soft underbelly of souvenir gift shops on the *Via Cavour.* He passed up one of the roads leading to his hotel, stopping off at a mini-supermarket and buying a can of soda, some cigarettes, a bottle of regular strength aspirins – and heading back to the hotel. Ignoring the elevator, he walked up the four flights to his room, gripping the bannister and moving quickly, purposely, pausing at infrequent intervals to catch his breath and listen to the early noises of sleeping buildings. He made it to the fourth floor, entered his room, and slumped down on the lower end of the bed. He sat there, on the lower end of the bed for about an hour, feeling tired, hungover, his stomach heaving and his head thumping queasily. He stared catatonically at the tapestries on the walls – the cherubs and titans, sportive nymphs and satyrs, the bull and lion locked in their eternal death struggle. He felt a terrible loneliness, as if the bottom had dropped out of his heart. His emotions were raw. He wanted to cry, but was afraid that if he started, he would never stop. He reached over the bed and picked up his university copy of Virgil's *Aeneid*, opening it and letting it fall randomly on a page. His eyes went to a line at the bottom.

What place on earth is not full of our sufferings? There are tears of things and mortal things touch the mind.
There was a brief quickening of the pulse, the lines echoed within him. He shoved himself off the bed, threw the book on the floor and walked over to his travel bag. He started rummaging through the bag, pulling out a series of different coloured bottles, small, large, green, yellow, orange, all with their own individual labels –a varied collection of leading pharmaceutical companies. He had everything, at least everything that was non-prescriptive: Dyclonine, Phenol, Acetaminophen, Ibuprofen, Naproxen, Doxylamine; Dextromethorphan. It had taken him a while to collect them. After leaving university, he'd

48

gotten the early train down to Dover, went into town and stacked up as best he could, hitting every chemist and pharmacist in the area, even going as far as Folkestone. It had taken him nearly six hours to collect them all. Then in a last-minute rush he had gotten a taxi down to the Dover docks and caught the night ferry over to Calais. You couldn't blame him for what he had done. There was just no going back from certain things. He had known from the moment Dr. Barnard had looked at him in that way that it was over; that he was finished, ended – kaput. It was hard to explain how he knew, but he knew. The way she had given him that contemptuous look of hers, the edges of her mouth pushed upwards and nostrils curled unnaturally inwards, gazing at him with a look of such unflappable superiority that it seemed to spring from some near total detachment and antipathy. He knew there was no going back from that look, no escaping that face, and so he had decided to up and leave, get himself out of there, take himself off to Rome and check himself out of life. It didn't seem too bad an end in the circumstances. One had to realise ones limitations, to accept that one had tried ones best, resign oneself to ones lot and, like Socrates, drink ones hemlock without complaint. His preferred hemlock was a bottle of *Cutty Sark* he had purchased at Dover. He had it all planned out. He would choose a night in Rome where he was ready, break the cap of the *Cutty Sark,* and start drinking slowly, moderately, enough to bring about a warm rosiness to the cheeks, a mild intoxication to the body, a stable anaesthetization turning gradually paralytic throughout the evening. He would take a bottle of the coloured pills, fill a glass with the whiskey and, supping on the whiskey, swallow the pills in handfuls of ten. There would be a lot of dancing about the hotel room, a lot of swaying and bending, squatting and shouting, tumbling and dipping and twisting and coming back up; trying ambitious turns, losing balance, falling, laughing, croaking –dying. It would be the perfect end in light of recent events, an appropriate final solution to an overly sensitive, hyper self-critical life. And what better place to do it in than Rome. The ancient Romans had fallen on their swords or, at best, cut their wrists in hot baths, but he –being too much a child of the twentieth-century –would take a lethal excess of modern therapeutic substances, a great contemporaneous quantity of sedatives and antidepressants and slide away into an inner dream, drift across the tranquil, still sea towards Virgil's netherworld. He knew he wasn't alone in such fantasies; history was peppered with similar individuals wanting to take themselves off to Rome to perform such noble acts, to become in their minds part of the buried stratigraphy of the vestigial ruins of the city. He *knew* he wasn't alone, same as he knew Mandii knew she wasn't alone. He had recognized it in her the first moment her saw her in the bar; those dark sullen eyes, that distant abstract look. He knew that look. It was the look of a dreamer, a fantasist, a romanticist, a person who lived in a world of ideas rather than objects, a person who had been to a million places in their head, happiest when left alone, and ready to entertain themselves with the toys of their own imagination. Maybe it was better to live that way, especially if the world wasn't giving you what you wanted. Maybe it was better to lose your grip on reality if things didn't work out, retreat into a world of fantasy to such an extent that you were unable to distinguish anymore between what was real and what was illusion –*maybe,* but he doubted it. Life was more than our idealisms of it. Reality intruded itself upon us, demanding to be listened to, causing a conflict between our idealised images and how they stood in brutal fact. All our comforting fallacies ultimately failed us, even our fallacies of death. The Protestant Cemetery had taught him that much. Sooner or later you had to face the world as it was, had to face that your old habits were no longer adequate, that your old needs were no longer satisfying, and that you were just another poor forked being in the world, another weak and restless creature, a human animal in all its messy, sticky, gooey nature; fragile, flawed, doubt-ridden, and anxious, holding onto its existence by its fingernails and seeking forgiveness. In the end we all turned relentlessly away from our dreams and back to the tears of things which the flesh inherited.

He didn't move for the rest of the day, but sat on the lower end of the bed, hugging the bottle of pills, slumped in an access of exhaustion as he watched the day through the shutters turn from white to violet. The tapestries melted in shades of orange and pink, and the room became bathed in shadows, the only light coming from the slender villa on the Quirinale Hill, a splash of color in the emptiness.

Jack Gilford! he thought. *I'm sure that was his name, the guy in 'The Love Boat' episode– Jack Gilford!*

The
African Girl

It was still hard to believe how he'd got here, the strange circumstances that led him several days earlier to this sleazy spot in the north. After what had happened, he had kept touching things; chairs, walls, tables, his mother and father, to make sure everything was real, that it wasn't all a dream. It was still a little hard to tell. He had left his house in Claygate early Friday morning and gotten into his car (a forty-year-old black Porsche with a missing rear bumper) –thrown his holdall on the back seat, turned the ignition, and headed north on the M1. Most of the drive north was trouble-free, moving at a comfortably 70 in the outside lane, passing industrial towns, factories, steelworks, expanses of terraced houses, the furnace stacks issuing white plumes of smoke into the air, soiling the sky. He left the M1 at Doncaster, passing beneath the motorway and taking the signs for Scarborough, arriving there around noon. The place he was staying at was at the end of a one-way street in the old part of town, a B&B Guesthouse-Pub with withering flowers in the window and painted gnomes in the front garden. Hardly a soul was inside the pub, just a few oldsters talking in soft tones and staring glumly into their ales. He took his key from the publican and headed up to his room. His room was small, acceptably decorated, if rather plain, with a single bed, old-fashioned wardrobe closet, table, phone, little bathroom behind. Beside the window was a garish watercolor of a woman, a dark gypsy nude in an attitude of repose, with solid legs and large cumbersome breasts. He crossed the room and stared at the watercolor, then stared out the window. The sun was almost down, a vivid orange slice above the horizon to the left of the castle, the wintry sea beyond. He went to his holdall and took out a bottle with a few inches of whiskey left in it. He opened the bottle, tilted his head, and took a slug. He carried a chair over to the bed and dragged his holdall up beside it. He rummaged in the holdall, took out an old leather box, pulled back the lid of the box, and retrieved a parcel of photographs. He loosened the parcel and withdrew a small picture, a two-by-four snapshot, placed the rest of them back in the box and regarded the picture. The picture was wrinkled and bent, sun-bleached and damaged with the passing of time. It displayed a boy sitting on a lakefront dock, waving gaily at the camera. He dug in the holdall and came out with a new bottle of whiskey. He broke the seal of the bottle, unscrewed the cap, and dropped the cap on the floor. He propped the picture against a pillow on the bed, put his feet up on the mattress, and settled back in the chair, looking at the picture and drinking in slow, steady swallows. Around seven or thereabouts, he went for a walk, making his way towards the underside of the cliffs. He passed up a series of lanes and cobbled walkways, moving past pebbledash terraces and Edwardian houses, mostly made into flats and private hotels. Young people hung around in clusters, drinking and hollering, girls in tight-fitting skirts and boots, boys in track-suits, little caps, bits of jewelry, the fake tan of the girl's legs hiding the goose bumps from the cold weather. He came to a pub on the corner of an estate block. A sign hung over the porch of the pub, hand-painted and weathered by sea and wind –*The Queen Anne*, *Live Sport & Exotic Dances.* A close-circuit camera pointed onto the street, and a doorman stood on the steps, a meat slab of a man covered in tattoos and knife scars.

'You been here before, pal?' the doorman asked. He said he hadn't.

'£3 admission, and no touching the girls.'

He paid the admission, gave the doorman a reticent smile, and passed into the pub. The inside of the pub was warm and spacious, brightly lit by electricity and done out in camp Victorian detail. Long black velvet drapes hung from the windows. There was a scattering of mock-antique tables and chairs. Near a mirrored wall was a stage with three chrome poles surrounded by mushroom stools, the edges decorated with black wrought-iron railings, the railings interspersed with fake brassy ornaments. Men stood around in groups of three or four, young lads in builders' attire, stone-faced men with their noses in papers, middle-aged crew-cutters with football shirts riding their soft, distended guts. The men fell silent as a girl walked in from a side-door. She was young and shapely, early twenties, garbed in black stockings and a semblance of a skirt, with a slight snub nose and large white spun-sugar wig rolled high above her head. She paraded through the pub, beaming a smile, sharing looks with her favorite punters, mounting the stage and preparing herself at the pole. The music began, and she started working the pole, grinding lewdly against it, bashing out a routine to some gooey love song from the 70s. She moved towards the center of the stage and leaned forward, revealing the shapely muscles of her thighs. The men looked on at her, paying little attention to the music, fixing their quick, dark eyes on her shapely thighs, the breasts looming high and resolute over the narrow waist. She began to disrobe, wiggling out of the skirt, pulling a shoulder strap free and letting her left breast pop out, then, reached down and stretched the crooked elastic of her panties. Her navel came into view, and an instant later, the top of her muff, flaxen and flat, like an expensive linen towel. She stood there for several seconds, naked from the waist down, staring with a certain arrogance, a hint of mockery, basking in the admiration of the craving eyes. She noticed a man a little ways' down from the poolroom, partly concealed by the standees, someone she hadn't seen there before. He was in his late forties, handsome but in a dissolute way, with prickly stubble and head of hair as red as a carrot. He watched her without so much as a smile or affirmation, sipping his beer and playing with a tower of coins he had stacked on the bar beside him. There was something about him, she thought, something in his ruffled demeanor, his posture, the way he was leaning against the bar, slumped almost, hugging himself, clutching his coat to his body like a vagabond, his grey turtleneck sweater pulled up to his chin and a graze on his left cheek. She did a twirl, facing towards the mirror, head down, hands pressed against the glass, feet straddled as she ground out a rhythm to the 70s love song. She continued staring at the man through the reflection in the mirror. He had nice eyes, she thought, eyes that didn't follow her around the stage like the others, eyes that didn't undress her, as if staring at a realness, an authenticity, an unhidden beauty that went beyond the length of her leg, the thrill of her costume. She did a turnaround, facing back towards her audience, her spun-sugar wig falling from its rolled-up position on her head and sweeping over her face like a glossy white veil. She pulled back the wig. Her eyes met the man's. She searched his face. She felt a fleeting impulse to touch his unshaven cheeks. He smiled back, wanly.

☐

'It's true!'
'No.'
'I'm telling you.'
'No, no.'
'Didn't you see her tonight, the one in the pink G-string with blonde extensions?'
'Which one?'
'What?'
'Which one, there were two in pink G-strings with blonde extensions.'
'The one with the pelican tattoo on her shoulder.'
'Right.'
'The one with the bouncy backside.'
'Right.'
'The one that was shooting ping pong balls between her legs into that fellas pint glass.'
'So, what about her?'
'Well, she's what I've been saying –she's one of them.'
'One of what?'
'One of *them,* known for breaking the champagne room rule for the right price.'
'So, what you're telling me is she does extras?'
'Yeah.'
'Put there by the pub owners to pull in the punters?'
'Yeah, and yeah.'
'I would never have guessed.'

'Well, it's true.'

'You don't mind that kind of thing then?'

'Why should I? If a girl wants to show her nanny-nanny to the world and shag the customers' that's her business. I've put up with worse, like the tossers that come in just to take the piss outa' you and tell you your trash. My personal favorites are the ones that look like they've stumbled in by accident while trying to find the library or church; drop their money into your pint glass at arm's length like they might catch a fatal disease from you or somert. Bloody tossers! I mean there I am, flashing my tits and unveiling my clit and all they can do is read their shitty *Sun* and give you funny looks. You know some bloke come up to me the other week and said, 'girls' like you are asking for it' –fuckin' twat I said to him, I mean I'm no bra-burning feminist but comments like that really get on me tits! I mean whose business is it how I addle me brass, why shoulda' girl worry about getting raped or killed all because she flashes her tits n' vagina for a livin? Pff!'

She rolled onto her back and stared up at the ceiling, shaking her great smiling face as though to an atrocious but funny joke. She continued staring at the ceiling, hiccupping and laughing, observing the strange shifting's of light and shadow made by the passing cars on the street below.

'Me sister says I should pack the job in,' said, her eyes following the patterns of light and shadow like a child watching fireworks. 'Says I'm better than that, constantly telling me en' all, always coming round or hassling me on t' fern.'

'Fern?'

'Yeah fern.'

'Huh?'

'Fern, smart-fern.'

'Oh, *phone*.'

'Oh, aye … sorre, I know, it's me accent en't it. It's a bit broad Yorkshire. Everyone that's got it sounds major thick … well … I'm not actually thick … well … I s'pose I'm a chav because of the way I talk … well … I'm not really a chav it's just that I'm from North Yorkshire. Liam says I should pack the job as well.'

'Liam?'

'The bloke I'm seeing –sorta, nice lad; works as a plumber down Garfield Road. He's with his pals at moment in Amsterdam on a stag do –dirty lil' boggers! Still, if that's what they like. Did you say you were married?'

'Divorced.'

'What happened?'

'It didn't work out.'

'Oh, I'm sorre. I don't think I'll get married y' know; cleaning backsides, watching daytime television, and cooking lasagna ain't my idea of fun. Me sister says it's cuz I'm a Sagittarius, y' know, free spirit, goes an' does what they pleases. When she was my age all she wanted to do was find the right man, put roof o'er her head an' three square meals on t' table. But that's not for me I say to her. I'm not like that I tell her. Not this girl. She s'all right, though –me sister, in her own way, very sound, works as a shampooer in salon up high street. She shampooed the hair of Jane McDonald the other week y' know.'

'Really.'

'I mean who would've reckoned, Jane Mc-bleeding-Donald in me sisters' salon. She was doing some charity event at the theatre and needed a blow-dry and set. She's shampooed quite a few celebs hairs me sister, in fact. She'll shampoo your hair if you want.'

'No, you're all right.'

'Put you in a few highlights, copper, blonde?'

'It's fine.'

'Maybe a cut an' comb?'

'Thanks.'

The girl laughed again and sat up, placing her long flaxen wig back on top of her head, positioning it as she twitched her nose at the weaves and fibers. She noticed a small snapshot on the bedside table. She leaned over and picked up the picture. 'Is this you as a lad?' she asked, staring at the small creased photo of a child beside a lake.

'Yes.'

'Aww, you look *so* cute! I hate looking at pictures of meself when I was a sprog. Too many teeth n' braces. Me mouth looked like a silver mine. You should put it on Facebook y' know.'

'No.'

'You should do.'

'I don't think so.'

'Why not?'

'Because I don't *want* to!'

He looked away from her, puzzled and angry at her questions. There was a strained silence. Her head went down, eyes blinking fast, trying to think of something to ease the tension, to make the silence go away.

'Charlotte Whattingham used t' stalk people on Facebook,' she said.

'What?!'

'Charlotte Whattingham, used t' stalk people on Facebook. Another girl I know, Janet Hague –well, I wouldn't really call her a mate –more like a slag –used to stalk one of my exe's for like six months. I stalked a bloke once meself; Christopher Chumley it was; thought he was the best thing in trousers; long dark locks, eyes as blue as the sea, six-pack like Patrick

Swayze. Then one day he sent me a message saying, 'comment on me profile picture again and I'll fuck you over' -*knob'ead*! Still, I didn't reckon his six-pack that much anyway, looked like uneven cobblestones down an alleyway.'

She rubbed her nose, rolled onto her stomach, and raised herself onto her elbows so that her face was close to his. 'So,' she went on, her long flaxen wig sliding over one eyebrow, 'tell me about yerself'

'What would you like to know?'

'I don't know; somert you haven't told me already.'

'There isn't much to say.'

'There must be somert.'

'Not much.'

'Well, where are you from?'

'A place called Claygate, in Surrey.'

'Oh! That sounds posh that does; is that where you got that nice accent from?'

'No, that was from boarding school.'

'Where, in Claygate?'

'No, Scotland.'

'Funny place to go to school if you're from south. So, what do you do?'

'I'm a solicitor.'

'Oh, one of those trip-over-and-sue-me-merchants are ya?'

'You could say that.'

'Is that why you're in Scarborough – soliciting?'

'No, I'm visiting somewhere for my holidays.'

'Where's that then?'

'Somewhere from long ago … a long time ago.'

Silence fell. In the shadows a spider appeared on the table, scurrying across the surface, moving fast to escape back into the shadows. He reached over to get rid of the scuttling intruder.

'Don't kill it!' she said.

'No?'

'Put it in t' bin.'

'Why? It's going to die in there isn't it?'

'I know, but don't kill it. When I see people squash bugs' I always think the same thing.'

'What is it you think?'

'I always think, how would they like it if they were a bug. I mean who knows; they might even come back one day as a bug and say, I don't like bugs' and squash their blinkin' selves –then where would they be.'

He shook his head, amused at her naivety and simplemindedness. 'Ursula,' he said, 'that's your stage name, I presume.'

'No, it's me own. I'm named after Ursula Andress, me mam used to think she was beautiful. She must've seen her in *Dr No* about seven hundred times, including *Casino Royale* about half as much.'

He smiled softly. 'You're a sort of scatterbrain, aren't you Ursula?'

'Yes, but I'm cute with it.'

She moved down the bed towards him, stroking her neck. 'It's late,' she said. 'I shan't think they'll have any taxis around this time. Looks like I'll have to stay here with you.'

He looked at her, slightly taken. 'Here! You mean as in *here!*'

'Yes, unless there's a stable you wish to put me in.'

He eyed her. She gazed at him, evenly, breathing heavily, her chest rising and falling, the bosom combining the fullness of a mature sensual woman and the resiliency of an adolescent. She shook her head, her white spun-sugar wig falling down, revealing a flowing mane of black curls which tumbled about her shoulders. He looked away, abruptly, nervously.

'As it being late,' he started. 'I suppose you shall have to stay here with me tonight.'

She smiled, fighting down an instinct to laugh. 'I shall like that *rather* much,' she said, mocking his accent. 'I shall like that rather much, indeed … Rupert! May I come to you?'

'As you like.'

She leaned forward and kissed him, lightly brushing her lips with his own, then rolled over, scratched her nose, and fell immediately to sleep. He took off his coat, put it over her feet, tossed the spider into the bin, and leaned against the headboard. He remained there for an hour, staring at the nude gypsy on the wall, listening to the surf outside the window, its sound like tumbling thunder, like distant cannons being fired. His hand went to the table, feeling the small photo he had placed there. He moistened his lips, half aware of something, something from the past, nearly forgotten, at the fringe of memory. For a moment his face went soft. He seemed to be able at last to picture exactly what he wanted.

It was a dark, overcast morning in Scarborough. The sun shone weakly through the trees, and a thin chill wind cut through the clothes of the early morning strollers. Small collections of jumble and dust glowed under the fragile cowardice of the streetlights, and seagulls could be seen landing across the resort, from the crumbling hotels to the rundown theatres on the front.

Rupert checked his watch –seven past seven. He yawned, rose from the bed, and crossed to the window.

He looked out at the silent streets. The moon had gone, but the stars were still out, the long dawn shadows lying thick and heavy across the roads and gardens. He turned from the window and walked into the bathroom, stealing a glance at Ursula as he passed by the bed. She was on her back, her arms outstretched, head turned to the side, hair framing it like a dark halo. He entered the bathroom, pulled some toilet paper from its rack, blew his nose and dropped the soggy paper into the toilet. He began to brush his hair, studying himself in the mirror as he did. He'd put on a few pounds that had rounded his face, and there was some lines about the eyes. Aging, he knew, was going to come on fast in the next few years. And yet he had good shoulders, and his hips and belly were heavy but solid. His hair was thick on his chest and across his back, and in the morning light some of it glowed a soft copper-red, like fox fur. He turned on the tap and filled the sink, cupped his hands and splashed the water on his face.

Ursula lifted her head from the pillow at the sound of the running water. She rubbed her eyes, moved her tongue around her mouth, stared blurrily at the crumpled snapshot on the table. Beside it was a phial of pills. She leaned over and picked up the phial, looking at the label.

ZERICONAL: ONE AT BEDTIME NEEDED FOR SLEEP.

'Rupert!' she called out. No answer. For a moment she thought he had gone out, but then his shabby overcoat was still hanging on the chair. 'Rupert,' she repeated, directing her voice to the partly open door of the bathroom. 'Hey Rupert! I was wondering what you're doing today. I think it's gonna be nice out.'

The water continued running.

'I thought we might go out for breakfast. I know this lil' caf' on t' sea; we could have a walk around; visit the castle, get some cockles. I'll show you Scarborough, I mean that's if you want to … me show you Scarborough?'

The toilet flushed.

'Well?'

The silver waves climbed higher on the long, thin beach. The lights of the amusement arcades shone garishly in the morning greyness, the one-armed bandits and penny slot consoles lit-up, gaudy, neon flashing and winking. There were a few deck chairs already out, a few wind breakers with some hardy souls under blankets. Street-sweepers removed the traces of the late-night revelry, and the gulls circled the lighthouse, their wings rising around the tower like a halo of white and blue.

Rupert and Ursula made their way along the promenade, passing ice cream parlors and seafood stalls. They came to a café near the fairground, entered, and moved towards a vacant table, ordering a pot of tea with chips and bread. Ursula licked her lips as the food arrived. She picked up the tomato-shaped plastic ketchup bottle and started squeezing its contents over her and Rupert's chips.

'Thank you,' said Rupert.

'And a bit o' vinegar?'

'No.'

'Here'

She picked up the vinegar bottle and added it to the already saturated chips, then, grabbing a handful of her own chips, inserted the chips between two pieces of thin white bread. She started eating noisily, greedily, putting it away quickly, talking fast. 'Nothing like a chip cob to bring you back to the land of the living,' she said. 'Best cure for a hangover *ever*. Maddy's favva swears blind that the best cure for a hangover is a hot bath with five tea spoons of mustard thrown in … oofh! I want a cure for a hangover, not feel like a piece of marinated ham.'

'You come down here a lot?'

'Every weekend, I've almost got me own table. I used to come here as a sprog with me mam and favva, that was before me favva went away.'

'Where did he go?'

'Don't know, he used to send us money from time to time, but we never saw him again. There's nowt much to say about him really. I *think* I remember him; it's hard to tell. I've seen pictures of him so I don't know if I remember seeing *him* or just *seem* to remember seeing him from all the times I've looked at the pictures. Nannan Gee told us that he had to go away, to be by himself. I don't know the reason, but something happened to him that made him want to get away from everything; or maybe he was just that way all the time. Like I say, we never did see him again.'

Rupert sipped his tea and gazed out the window. In the harbor the fishermen were putting out their nets. Small boys were lobbing stones at pieces of flotsam bobbing in the incoming water.

'You like living in Scarborough?' he asked.

'Is'll right,' she said. 'Being a Scarborian means that you get to know everyone else's business which can kinda get on ya nerves. People around here tend to get a bit petty about things, y' know, can be a bit small minded, think Custard Creams are the height of cuisine and working for £4 an hour in a hotel is a career. But I suppose it's not too bad a place really. At least people greet one another in t' street, which is more than I can say for some places. I'm not too fond of the beach though. I don't think the sea agrees with me. Me mam used to douse me and ah Sonia in baby oil, which had no sunscreen. We were like two fried chickens by end of day – and the sandwiches! Bloody nora! What is it with sandwiches on t' beach? No matter how much you wrap them in cellophane they're always crunchy with sand!' She stopped eating and wiped her full red face with a napkin. Her lips shone with the grease from the chips. 'I remember,' she continued, 'when me Auntie Abel fell off donkey ride on beach –blew her knee out in six different places … spent six months in traction, poor dear. The day she came out hospital she went walking up high street and caught her plastered leg in wheel of butcher's cart. It was a right scene. She was stuck there all day. She wasn't goin further in any direction, no way, no how. In the end we had to push n' pull her big behind up street with cart attached. All you could hear was a bunch of panting an' gasping and grunting coming from behind cart, broken by the occasional … let's be avin' ya Abel, and, c'mon Abel, and you can do it Abel and alright Abel.'

Rupert finished his tea and poured another. Ursula squinted, studying his profile as he stared out the window.

'So, what about you?' she asked.

'About me?'

'What you were saying last night, the reason you're in Scarborough?'

'It's a long story.'

'Well, gimme the highlights.'

'Look, Ursula … you're a nice girl, but you don't want to get involved with me.'

She tossed her head and let out a laugh as if she had heard something ridiculous. 'Oh, go on with ya!' she

said. 'You'd think I'd asked you to go out looking for rings or somert. Anyroad, I said I was going to show you Scarborough, so I'm bloody well going to show you Scarborough, aint I? … right?'
Rupert rendered her a sheepish smile and looked down at a spatter of ketchup on his trousers.

They made their way around the bay, passing rock pools and beach huts, some weathered summer homes. The shore was a graceful arc of sand, stretching away in a gentle curve towards the tip of the sea. The beach was made up of flat, hard pebbles, with occasional tufts of withered grass, and behind these, behind the summer homes, bracken-covered cliffs rose, disappearing into a dark cascade of trees. Rupert walked at a steady pace while Ursula strode several paces in front of him, whistling through her teeth as she gathered seashells and colored stones. She was like a schoolgirl on holiday, bouncy and uninhibited, her hair sweeping back and smiling into the wind, the salty air.
'I love mornings like this,' she said. 'Not too parky, but enough for a light jacket. They always make me feel good about things. You know, I woke up the other morning and felt happy. I just woke up and there I was happy, and not just a little bit happy, but *seriously* happy … happy with the world … happy with the trees … happy with the sea … happy with the hills and sky and clouds … and it wasn't even a nice day, in fact it was pissing it down, and there I was walking along in the piddlin' rain in this little jumper and a scarf and all I could think about was how happy I was. It was like I couldn't tell you why I was happy, I had no reason *not* to be happy, but at the same time I didn't have a reason *to* be happy –I was just happy. I saw this programme once that said people aren't as happy as animals. Did

68

you see it? It had those animals in it –what are they called?'

'What?'

'The animals in Australia, the ones with the big black noses that look like little bears'

'Koalas.'

'Aye, this programme said they were the happiest animals alive it did. It has to do with their diet or somert. Apparently, they eat this plant that makes them happy, somert called –apocalyptus. '

'Eucalyptus.'

'Right, an' they eat this plant and it kinda zones them out. Liam tried to get hold of some the o'er week but couldn't find any local dealers.'

She turned and faced Rupert, stopping him as he waked up a sand dune.

'Look,' she said, 'I don't really know you, Rupert. In fact, I don't know you at all, but I trust you. I usually don't get that wi' men. There's this place I'd like to show you, a place that's important to me.'

'Listen, Ursula –'

Not letting him finish, she leant forward and put a finger against his lips. 'C'mon,' she said, grabbing him by the arm and leading him up the beach.

They started away from the shore, passing some tall sea grass and taking a path up the cliffs. The cliffs rose steeply, cut out by deep chasms and towers of bracken. In places the bracken was dense, growing up and through and branches of trees, hanging indiscriminately in great ragged curtains over their heads. Rupert tried to ignore the ache in his knees as he climbed, bracing his feet against the loose soil, grabbing handfuls of bracken for support, gulping down air and groaning it out. On the upper side of the cliffs the land flattened out, and there, against the glowing breast of the sky, was a secluded shelter, a small Victorian arbor commanding a magnificent view of the harbor. Rupert followed Ursula into the arbor. They sat staring at the sea. They chose to be silent.

Ursula reached into her handbag and took out a packet of cigarettes. She handed one to Rupert, put one in her mouth, and lit them both up. 'I used to come here as a kid,' she said, dragging deep on the cigarette. 'It was my little hiding place away from the world. After me favva left, me mam used to entertain different fellas. She was a strange old bird me mam; thought more of her boyfriends than she did her own daughters. I would come up here to get away from things at home. You can't blame her for the way she was really. Poor cow was pregnant at thirteen. She never stood a chance in life. Her liver looked like a Spotted dick pudding in the end from all the drink. You've heard the joke about alcoholics aintcha?'

Rupert shook his head.

'A man asks an alcoholic what are the benefits of being sober?'

'What did he say?'

'I don't know.'

'I don't get it.'

'Never mind.'

They both stared at the sea. A wind rose up over the cliff and approached them carrying salt spray. The spray passed over the arbor, passed over the walled gardens, the houses, over the graveyards with their withered tombs. The cheerful countenance on Ursula's face had diminished somewhat. It was hard to tell whether it was from the shadows or her mood. She finished her cigarette, taking one last quick drag, and stubbing it out under her heels, twisting it fiercely under her leopard print ankle boots.

'I had a place like this,' said Rupert.

Ursula looked up from her boots, turning her head towards him. Rupert leant forward, wiping his heavy red hair from across his eyebrows. 'It's strange to talk about it after all this time,' he said, 'I must have been four when it happened. We were on holiday in Yorkshire somewhere. There was this old ruined church, a large gothic structure with a sloping lawn out back. A stream ran away from the church, misty-white in color, pearly white, like the subtle sweep of a painters' brush.' He paused, drawing deep on his cigarette. 'I followed the stream, treading through the grass, passing smooth lawns and garden houses. The stream bore right, then left, around hills, under bridges. On I went, disappearing with it into the trees. Suddenly something flashed through the leaves of the trees ...' He hesitated, gazing at the sea, at the distant horizon. 'It was a lake,' he went on, 'a large shining lake. It broadened out from the trees, becoming vaster and vaster, extending into wider and wider views, parts of it in yellow, other parts in blue shadow.' He smiled at the remembrance, and his eyes grew larger. 'It must have been at least twenty acres, deep as it was wide, with swans all over it, hundreds and hundreds of swans. They filled the lake, crowding it –like a sea of silvery-white snow. I remember looking out towards the other side of the lake, past the swans. It was heavily wooded there, with new spring leaves, steeper, denser, and with foliage … I think there was a mariner over there … I think there was some people there … I think they were laughing.' He stopped suddenly. The ash broke from his cigarette and fell to the ground. He seemed to take stock, his full pink lips slightly parting, and he relaxed those tight hands on the cigarette. Out to sea, a ship slid towards the land, its fog horn long and haunting. 'My world's been falling apart, Ursula,' he said, 'things that once made sense to me don't make sense anymore. I thought that if I found this lake things would change … that I could be myself again … that everything would work out –do you understand that?'

Ursula stared at him, her expression mystified and slightly fearful. Beyond the bay floated a border of pale sunlight. The light reached the rocks below them, turning pink and mauve as it touched the arbor.

☐

'Ursie, what are you playing at?'

'Nothing, I'm playing at nothing.'

'It doesn't look like that to me.'

'What's that supposed to mean?'

'I've had Liam on the phone all morning. He said you haven't been answering his calls.'

'Well, I haven't.'

'Fer Chrissakes, Urs!'

'What?'

'You know how that boy feels about ya.'

'Oh, I'm not sure.'

'I am. He'll give his right arm for ya.'

'Do you really think he likes me that much?'

'A blind man on a galloping horse can see that he does. The dozy beggars' like a love-struck puppy dog. It'll break his heart if he hears you been knocking about with another fella.'

'I aint knocking about with anyone.'

'Then who's this bloke I been hearing about?'

'Eh?'

'This scruffy bloke you met last night down that sleazy place you work?'

'Oh, aye. News travels fast don't it. Maddy been around has she?'

'No, in fact it was Mrs. Briggards. Our Lucy bumped into her down Iceland's this morning; said she saw you walking down promenade with your new fella.'

'That woman has a bigger mouth than an alligator.'

'Well, I'm not here to tell you what to do. I just think you should act a little responsibly sometimes. I mean ain't you got any consideration for Liam?'

'Liam an' me aren't joined at the hip you know. Christ, I've only been going with the lad for a month. I don't see what all the fuss is about.'

'Maybe we're worried about you, Urs, maybe we're worried about you acting the loose cannon all the time, being the party-girl, throwing up in curbs, doin' lines of coke in pub toilets, larkin' about with whoever happens to be around an' flashing yer tits for a livin'.'

'Oh, here we go.'

'I mean you just can't seem to commit to nowt, whether it be a decent job or another human being. I've lost count o' times I've seen you walking down promenade still in yer party clothes with some new fella on yer arm.'

'Pack it in!'

'Maybe we're worried about you going the way of ah mam, sleeping with whomever takes ya fancy, getting yourself pregnant by some half-wit who does a runner at the first sign of adulthood and leaves you a single-parent to bring up two kids and drink yourself into an early grave.'

An audible sob could be heard coming from the other end of the phone.

'Look, Sonia,' said Ursula. 'I've got to go now … I'll phone you later.'

'Phone Liam as well.'

'I will.'

Ursula pressed the hang up button, diverted her calls to voicemail, placed the phone in her bag, and walked back into the service station. She worked her way through the tables, coming to a table near the toilets. Rupert sat hunched over the table; fingers curved around a cup of tea as he stared sightlessly out at the traffic on the road.

'That was me sister,' Ursula said as she approached him. 'Just wondering how things are.'

No answer came from Rupert. She took a seat opposite him, resting her elbows on the table and her chin on her hands, watching him as he studied the road.

'Rupert,' she started. 'Do you mind if I ask you something?'

'If you wish.'

'Why did you marry?'

'The usual reasons: companionship, security, love, why do you ask?'

'It's just that you don't look like the married sort.'

'I don't?'

'You have a certain look to you.'

'I do?'

'I'd call it sensitive, uncertain –vulnerable.'

'You say it like it's a good thing.'

'It is. Vulnerability is *very* attractive in a man. At least that's what I think.'

Rupert's eyes resumed their trance-like stare at the road. Ursula bit her lip. She thought for a moment she had had no right to ask such a question. But she wanted to see what he would say. She was glad he had said he had married for love.

'If you want to know what I'm like in a relationship,' Rupert began, 'I'm the romantic type. Or *was*; the seeds are left –drying up, though.'

'Yeah, I can see that,' said Ursula. 'You being the romantic type, I mean you being of a certain age an' everything … well, what I mean is that you're probably old enough to remember when social intercourse didn't mean a quick bonk after the Bingo session; when people talked on trains with strangers because it was part of normal life. In a sense, I'm a bit like that myself – a bit old fashioned. When I was younger, I would hitch lifts with just about any car or lorry driver. None of whom, strangely enough, turned out to be a murderer or rapist. So why did you an' your wife breakup?'

'Too much quarreling and heartache. I knew there was something wrong when I came home one day and found her throwing everything out of the wardrobe; said she needed a new look. When the divorce papers finally came through, she referred to me as nice but *emotionally unavailable* –a psychological term.'

'Ouch.'

'She ended up moving to the south of France with her seventy-year-old fitness instructor. I haven't heard from her in four years.'

Rupert resumed his trance stared at the road. Ursula blew on her tea and followed his gaze. 'I don't think me and Liam will last,' she said. 'D'you know he got charged for possessing an offensive weapon and threatening someone with it – it was a rolling pin; he thought some bloke had sent me a picture text message of himself naked. I told him it wasn't true, but he wasn't havin' any of it. He was given a twelve-week prison sentence suspended for two years. He can be such a hashtag knob 'ead sometimes.' She picked up her cup, taking the tea in both hands and humming under her breath. 'But I don't mind him, though,' she went on. 'He turned up one Thursday night a month ago down the Queen Ann, said I was a bit of alright and that he would buy me a kebab and chips. Who could resist such an offer? Yeah, he's all right is Liam. It's just that it's a bad idea to date the customers. I mean who wants to get intimate with someone who's seen you starkers on the pub floor with your legs open for a quid … oh, I almost forgot,' she reached into her pocket and pulled out a keychain, with a small fob attached to the end; an ebony figure of a young girl. 'Present from t' shop,' she said, 'pretty, ain't it? I reckon it's African, like a good luck charm. I want you to have it. It might help you find your lake.'

Rupert stared at the small dark trinket. A flush rose to his cheeks. His face turned into a round grin.

'Thank you,' he said.

'Tha's alright,' she said. 'You know that's the first proper smile you've given me.'

'Is it?'

'You should do it more often. It suits you.'

Rupert finished his tea, and turned his eyes back to the road. 'Say, we better get going. There are a few places left to see that might be the lake.'

'Okay.'

'I mean; that's if you still want to.'

'I want to.'

'We could go back to Scarborough and I could do this another day.'

'I said I want to.'

He gave her another smile, but this time the smile quickly dissolved.

It was an imposing ruin, a commanding structure of the late medieval period. Lattice carvings hung above ornate doorways. Gargoyles and skulls peered from the tops of Romanesque columns. Cascades of masonry lay where they had fallen centuries before. The setting sun streamed through the upper windows, casting long beams of yellow light over the patches of grass. Rupert blinked dully at the light, and walked to the eastern window, laying his hands on the ancient altar. Beyond the altar lay a broad meadow, adorned with deer's and scattered oaks, and a little way off, a brook of sparkling water ran between banks, working its way across the land.

'What was it you said again?' asked Ursula.

'No swans,' said Rupert.

'I thought the website said there was.'

'Well, there isn't.'

'It said there was a canal with a footbridge.'

'That doesn't mean there are swans.'

'But don't swans hang around canals?'

'Yes, but they don't hang around *every* canal. They have different waterways and feeding grounds. Look it doesn't matter alright. I should've checked before we left.' He turned and looked at the broken masonry, gazing at the decaying elegance with a mixture of melancholy and disappointment.

'It's a bit quiet here, en't it,' said Ursula. 'Where're all the tourists gone?'

'It's past five,' said Rupert, 'they've probably gone back for the day.'

'That's a shame. I like seeing people enjoying these old places.'

'I prefer it when it's quiet.'

'You don't like people very much, do you Rupert?'

'They're alright. I just prefer it when they're not around.'

'That was the first thing I noticed about you –being on your own. It's hard to find someone on their own in Scarborough. Everybody's with somebody. You looked different, sitting there at the bar with your pint in your hand and your stack of coins –alone.'

'You felt sorry for me?'

'You just looked different. I suppose I wanted to see what you were about. People don't give each other enough chances in this life – and your eyes.'

'My eyes?'

'I liked your eyes. I don't know, it was their look or something in them, like I knew it or understood it or at least wanted to. I thought there was a lot going on behind those eyes.'

They both stood staring at the ruins, locked in mutual silence. Two pigeons darted out through a glassless window and disappeared. Ursula started moving around the columns, passing between the fallen stones, picking at the moss on the walls. 'I love places like this,' she said. 'I think it's cool that these stones have been here so long. I always thought at school that history was made-up, that it was all about imagining things, pretending something was real when it wasn't. I think different now. I think it was real, as real as you and me, that it was full of real people thinking real thoughts, dreaming real dreams, living real lives and dying in real beds. I sometimes think we have responsibility to those people, that without us they can't exist, that without our care they will disappear –like ghosts in the morning – d'you know what I mean?'

She turned to Rupert. He was staring upward, his eyes transfixed on something. There, near the chapter house, a flight of swan's were stretching their necks towards the western sky, riding the air in a billow of white and gold.

They left the abbey, taking a side door towards a sloping lawn below the eastern window. They crossed the lawn and made their way across a meadow, coming to the brook. They followed the brook for about a mile, entering a band of trees. They walked through the trees, walking under the curtains of branches. Ursula was out of her milieu, floundering along through the high vegetation in her leopard ankle boots, tripping and stumbling, cursing. They came to a footbridge flanked by two sphinx statues. On the left was a red-brick wall, and beside that, the remains of an old Victorian Hydro-electric generator. To the right, disappearing into the trees, could be seen a wire mesh fence, a caged door visible, with a metal sign nailed to the front, the lettering badly peppered with rust and generations of bird droppings.

LYNDE BASINS RESERVOIR
KEEP OUT

Rupert looked at the fence and back at Ursula, 'Think you can make it?' he said.

She gave him an accusing frown. 'In these heels?'

He ran a hand through his hair and started up the fence, wedging the toes of his shoes between the links. The fence seemed threc miles high, but he made it over and down the other side, dropping the last few feet. He walked back to where Ursula was, trying the handle of the door, drawing back the rusting bolt from the inside. They were standing in some sort of clearing. About twenty feet to the left the ground fell away from them, sloping into an irrigation ditch. A ribbon of water – the remains of the brook –moved sluggishly through bulrush and hyacinth. The other side of some trees could be made out a stretch of water, a line of dull purple on the far side of a motorway overpass. Rupert stepped through the trees and down towards the water, working his way towards its banks. He stopped at the edge of the water, stared around, then sat on a wooden beam that made a sort of curbing. Below, some thirty feet beneath was a kind of cement wall –a breakwater, frequented by moorhens and gulls, a thin scum of litter along the rim. Over the other side of the water was a warehouse, with an an outlet tower rising from the trees.

'This is it?' said Ursula –'an old reservoir?

Rupert didn't answer, but continued staring at the water.

'So, what are you going to do now?' Ursula asked.

'About what?' said Rupert.

'I mean now you've found this place?'

'Do I have to do anything?'

'Well, there's nowt 'ere but dirty water.'

'It's what *used* to be here.'

From the warehouse came the sound of clangs and scrapes of galvanized iron. The whirling of a conveyor-belt started up. A pair of swans came in, gliding over the dark sheet of water, flying low to watch the lonely ghosts of themselves that fled beneath them.

'Look,' said Ursula, 'I'm not being funny or anything, but now you've found this place it's best you moved on with your life. I understand you had a nice time here when you were a kid, but you can't get anything from this place now.'

Rupert didn't answer, but continued watching the water.

'What I'm trying to say,' she went on, 'is that the past is the past –yesterday's gone. Whatever you're looking for here ain't here anymore.'

Rupert turned and stared at her, his brooding eyes seeming to be fall out of his head with weariness and frustration. 'I see,' he said. 'And what are *you* looking for Ursula? A substitute father perhaps, someone to tell you you're not trash and that you weren't abandoned as a child. I don't need anybody's advice on what I should or shouldn't do, especially from some good time northern chav who takes her kit off for a living and has a father complex.'

Ursula took a step backward at his remark, staring at him wide-eyed, frozen and confused between tears and rage. 'Are you quite finished?' he said.

Rupert nodded that he had.

'Good! In the first place, *you* invited me along on this little outing as far as I remember. And second, who the hell do you think you're calling a chav? I may take my kit off for a living, but at least I have a life.'

'What, the Queen Ann? You call that a life?'

'It's better than moping around dreaming of some never-never land with lakes an' swans.'

'I'll stop dreaming when I'm ready, thanks.'

'You know something Rupert, all I've done is been nice to you and all you've done is treat me like a bag o' shite, well, let me tell you something luvvy, I've had enough of that treatment from men so I bloody well ain't gonna take it from you as well!'

There was a long, wounded pause. They regarded each other aggressively. The water lay still and dense.

After a moment's pause, Rupert said: 'Look Ursula, I can't do this.'

'Can't do this?' Ursula said, even more confused than ever. 'Can't do *what*?'

'I can't do this.'

'I'm not following.'

'This isn't my thing.'

'What?'

'This isn't my bag.'

'Rupert –'

' –isn't my idea of fun.'

'What are you talking about?'

'For God's sake, do you need it spelled out for you? I came here to kill myself … okay… you got it now … I want to kill myself here … You got it? Enough!'

There was a moment's stunned silence. Ursula's face went slack. Her mouth fell open, and she stared at Rupert, speechless. 'I believed you, Rupert,' she said, the tears beginning. 'I believed you when you said you were looking for somewhere that would make you happy, that would help you get back on your feet, put you in the right place, get you feeling yourself again, when all the while all I was doing was helping you do yourself in? Well –*fuck* you Rupert! I'm not helping anyone do themselves in. You can do that yourself!'

She turned and, without a backward glance, made for the fence in determined strides.

☐

Everything was dark. A quarter moon rose in the sky. From the trees came the first sorrowful, tender hoot of owls. The brook twisted across the land, the outlines of the ruined abbey no more now than a barely discernible silhouette against the horizon. Rupert sat hunched over the reservoir, hands clasping his knees, rocking slowly back and forth on his heels. He stared at the expanse of desert-like water. Memories crowded his head, images of swans, flowered wreathed banks, ghostly figures cloaked in summerwear. He breathed deeply and withdrew the bottle of whiskey from his coat pocket, unscrewed the top, took a long swallow, and waited till it hit. Then he took another swallow and set the bottle down in the dirt. Reaching in his pocket, he pulled out a small phial of pills. He stared at the phial, balancing it in his left hand, taking the bottle of whiskey and balancing that in the other, regarding them both. He placed the whiskey and pills back in his pocket, his fingers touching something else there. As he withdrew his hand, he saw it was the keychain Ursula had bought him in the service station. For long, silent moments he stared at the keychain thoughtfully, turning the small ebony figure over and over, studying the miniature carved African girl. His hands trembled. So did his upper lip and part of his chin.

A wind stole quietly over the water. An unknown light seemed to bathe the wasteland with a dull, inflexible glow. Imperceptibly, a silhouette appeared in the sky, an intense mass of light and dark shadow rising in the east so that in several minutes there was a pale glow above and behind the horizon. Straight lines of light fell to the water. It took up the whole of the space, bearing in the center of itself a long, coiling image of silver, a chill, bending flame. He craned his neck and stared up into the night sky. Eyes wide, he let his hands fall to his sides as he looked. He started to laugh, an insane laugh, a mirthless laugh, like his innards were falling out. He could see snowflakes –large white snowflakes, wafer-thin and phosphorus, floating down across the dark, naked water. It was like there had never been a dawn.

That gas cooker is in serious need of Marigolds, thought Ursula. In fact she thought the whole kitchen was in serious need of Marigolds. There was a ruddy old toaster crammed with something or other, a kettle that urgently needed de-scaling, a bin half-choked with eggshells and chicken carcasses. Rivulets of grease lined the walls, and on a window-ledge a comb with hair in it threw a long, tangled shadow. Ursula stood in the doorway to the dirty kitchen, staring at a pair of feet sticking out from under the sink.

'I didn't know you worked Sat'days?' she said to the feet, raising her voice as to shout over a portable radio blasting Hip-Hop music.

'Overtime,' said the pair of feet.

'So, what time you here to?'

'Till job's done.'

'Amsterdam sounded a good laff then, like I couldn't've guessed.'

The feet slid out from under the sink, followed by a dark hand gripping a pipe wrench. It was a young man, no more than twenty, of medium height and build, Afro-Caribbean, with a shaven head and green eyes set horizontally under a childlike face. He started wiping his hands on a cloth, looking Ursula up and down.

'T'was alright,' he said. 'So, what's goin' on, Urs, where you bin?'

'Around.'

'Maddy says you disappeared last night with some fella down the Annie.'

There was a pause.

'Well, is it true?'

The rattle and hum of the Hip-Hop music continued blaring, blasting its rhythmic urban tones so loudly that the small radio speaker rattled.

'Well, is it?'

84

Ursula averted her eyes from his. 'You knew what I was like before you asked me out Liam,' she said.

The young man turned, snapped off the radio, bent down and started clearing up some tools.

'Look, it wasn't anything,' Ursula explained. 'I didn't fancy him or anything. He was old enough to be me dad. I just felt sorry for him, is all.'

The young man continued clearing up the tools.

'We didn't do nowt,' she persisted, 'he just wanted to look around the Dales for this place he remembered as a kid.'

'Oh, aye, and I bet you helped him find it as well.'

'I *told* you we didn't do nowt! Jesus' sakes, he was twice me bloody age!'

He finished clearing up the tools, stood, and slung them over his shoulder, a look of confusion and irritation on his face. Ursula stared at him plaintively. 'I don't want to lose you, Liam,' she said, the frustration in her voice bringing tears to her eyes. 'I've lost enough people in me life, what with mam and dah, Nannan Gee just last year. I can't stand losing anybody else – can't *stand* it!'

She was shaking with sobs now, and the mascara ran down the side of her nose like wet paint. He walked over and wrapped an arm round her. 'C'mere ya daft thing,' he said, wiping the mascara from her nose with a finger. 'What we gonna do with you, eh?'

'You could always keep me locked up,' said Ursula, sniffling.

'Chained to the kitchen sink you mean?'

'I wouldn't mind.'

They stood for a moment, hugging each other, standing together in that small dirty kitchen, Ursula's head held in his hands, her black hair folded against his chest, her lashes wet, golden in the overhead light. He lifted her chin and kissed her on top of the head, then stood up, stiffened, and cleared his throat. 'Look, Urs,' he began. 'I was wonderin', what with us being together, being an item, sorta, well … er … I was wonderin' what you were doin' over the next sixty years?'

Ursula pulled away from him and stared incredulously. He coughed and said: 'I mean, how do you feel 'bout taking the plunge with a plumber?'

'Are you asking me to marry you?'

'Well … yeah, kinda, I mean get engaged first, married later, that's if you'll have me.'

'But we've only been going out for a month.'

'I know, but you know when you like someone … you just know …you know … you know when you want to take care o' them, spend time wi' them, do boring things like unload dishwasher.'

'Fill in tax returns.'

'Watch weekend television.'

'Repair ninety-degree bends.'

They laughed at their own jokes.

Ursula stepped into his arms again. He clasped her to him, reveling in the feel of her once more. He could feel her heart beating like a birds' against his chest. 'So, what's the answer?' he said.

Ursula looked down at her shoes, her cheeks flushing brick-red under the running mascara. She raised her chin and met his eyes with an upward glance that implied her answer.

'Do you think you'll be able to put up with a wayward woman like me?' she asked.

'I'll try,' he said.

The stripper looked like she knew how to work it. She was heavy-set, in her forties, rounded with age, yet moved with a certain graciousness, a sort of touching, coltish animation, different from the other more younger strippers. She draped her long blonde mane over her red shoulders, running it across her full bloated cleavage. Here and there were visible subtle imperfections, perhaps a line around the mouth of a misplaced pound, a stray glance or a stray pubic hair – she was all tits and tan lines. Every once in a while, she would flex her foot in its slipper heel, shoving the toe under one of her admirers at the front. 'Kiss, kiss,' she would lisp as the man cast his vulture-like eyes over her writhing behind and pubic beginnings –'Kiss, *kiss.*'

It was Saturday night down the Queen Ann and everyone was pretty oiled. Drunken youths fell about the place. Businessmen in gaudy suits danced with semi-clad girls half their age. The pub grunted, slapped, whistled. Light whimpered across the bodies. Drinking competitions were in operation; the Bee Gees sang *More Than a Woman* from the speakers, and on the large plasma screen Sheffield Wednesday was losing 2-1 to Cardiff City. Besides the gents toilets, sitting on a wine-colored sofa, old but in good repair, sat Ursula and her sister Sonia, Ursula in her black stockings and white spun-sugar wig and her sister dressed in plain jeans and a turtleneck sweater, the white spun-sugar wig of Ursula's rolled high above her head and balanced there.

'I can't believe it!' said Sonia in a fast, hard, slightly nasally voice, rapping the words out as though she were angry –'our own Ursie, getting hitched!'

'Engaged,' Ursula corrected her.

'Alright, engaged then. I remember when my Troy popped the question. It was after an all-day drinking session down the Conservative club. I said yes and he never remembered the next day. I wouldn't've minded, but I was five months gone at the time. So, who's this fella I been hearing about?'

'He was just some fella I met.'

'I heard he was something of a scruff.'

'I just like him, alright.'

'Liked him?'

'Yeah, liked him, is that against the law these days.'

'Maddy said he reminded her of that fella in that film.'

'What film's that then.'

'That film with Tom Cruise in it, the one where he's got the mentally retarded brother, dead serious, whatshisname … Dustin … Dustin Hoffman.'

'Rain Man.'

'Aye. Rain Man, he looked like Rain Man he did … drooling lips … knuckles dragging on t' floor, like that.'

'Maybe I fancied giving the older man a try before settling down.'

'Well, you coulda' picked a better one. Not exactly knight on white charger by the sounds of things, more like night of the living dead.'

The woman on stage was naked now, except for a pair of tight black leather panties. She put her knees together and pulled down the panties, exposing two tightly formed cheeks. The punters moved closer, pushing and shoving to get nearer the front of the stage. The woman smiled and flickered her ludicrously up-curling fake lashes. Some fat man, sweating bullets and swallowing them, leant forward and hollered: 'Wattaya got there – dried *shrimp?*'

'Look, what's bothering you, Urs?' Sonia asked.

'Nothing,' answered Ursula.

'Is it Liam?'

'No!'

'Is it something to do with this fella?'

'It's got nowt to do with him alright! I'm just pissed off is all!'

'Pissed off! About what? Getting married?'

'Yes, if you must know! I just wish I could've done something different with me life, something that didn't involve watching daytime television an' warming up chicken nuggets on a Saturday after football. I could've travelled a bit, seen the world, gone to college, you remember that time I wanted to be a beautician.'

'Sure I do, they wouldn't take you on the course.'

'I took me GCSE's didn't I?'

'Yeah, but you didn't pass 'em.'

'Well, maybe not that but something else then.'

'Listen, I know you, Ursie, I know what type o' girl you are. You're a free spirit, lives on a whim, goes where she pleases. When I was your age I'd had enough of hangovers' and one-night stands. All I wanted to do was settle down an' find the right man, one who could provide for me, put roof o'er me head an' three square meals on t' table. But you're not like me, you've got more brass than I had. I suppose that's why I was always afraid for you, afraid because I could see ah favva in you. I remember him y' know, you have the same eyes as him; sensitive, searching, trying to find their way home and not knowing where that home was or even if it exists.'

The two sisters stared at one another thoughtfully. The moment was broken by the sound of a man vomiting into a potted snake plant.

'Look,' said Sonia, 'whoever this fella is, if he's the one you want, then go to him. Just don't tell anybody I told ya so.'

Ursula gave her sister a trusting smile, rose from the sofa, and made for the door, zigzagging through the drunken men, purpose and haste in her stride. The stripper on stage wrapped up her dance by dropping to a squat, touching herself, putting a finger inside, smiling.

□

The night bore down fast upon Scarborough. The world had grown dark within the hour, heaven had blended with earth. Rupert made his way along the sea front. He walked with a monotonous rhythmic step, his head down, hands listless at his sides, passing shellfish stools, ice-cream parlors, rundown theatres. Crowds of youths hung about in clusters; girls pissed as farts and boys urinating down alleyways, most of them gravitating towards the promenade, being enticed by the siren-calls of the dance music and ringing of fruit machines that permeated the air, drifting from the arcades. He entered the pub he was staying at. It was quiet, the same bunch of regulars sitting at tables and staring glumly into their ales.

'Howdo?' the publican said as Rupert entered, greeting him with a warm but reserved smile.

'Room 111 please,' said Rupert.

The publican took Rupert's key from a rack and handed it to him.

'Do you know if there were any calls for me tonight?' asked Rupert.

The publican paged through some notes beside the till.

'Nothing, sir.'

'Messages?'

'Not to my knowledge, was you expecting any?'

'No, I suppose not. I'll have a large scotch.'

'Anything with it?'

'No, as it comes.'

The publican poured Rupert his scotch, eyeing him curiously from under his oversized bushy eyebrows.

'So, y' up here for holidays then?' he enquired.

'Sort of,' said Rupert.

'You'll like it up here. You know one of the Bronte sisters is buried in t' cemetery behind us?'

'Is that right.'

'Anne Bronte. They put a play on about her a few summers back at the open-air theatre; disappointing production though, not many people turned up for it. So, why you in Scarborough?'

'I like the sea. You know what they say; the sea washes away the stains and wounds of this world.'

'That's a nice saying.'

'It's Euripides.'

'Euripides! What's Euripides?'

'It's not a *what,* it's a he – a Greek playwright. I'll have another.'

'Closing time.'

'I'll be off to bed then.'

'Right you are, will you be wanting tea in your room t'morrow?'

'No thanks.'

'Right you are, g'night lad.'

Rupert swallowed the dregs of his scotch, slid off the stool, laid some money on the bar, and went upstairs without another word. In the room he slumped down on the bed. He pulled the bottle of whiskey from his coat pocket, unscrewed the top and took a slug. The whiskey

burned in his throat, trickling down through his chest –
like a small sun burning there. He crouched on the bed,
taking intermittent sips of the whiskey, the monotone
silence of the room surrounding him. Occasionally,
through the walls, could be heard the noise of the other
hotel guests: coughs, mumbles, doors shutting,
humping sounds. Slowly, wearily, stubbornly, he rose
from the bed and headed into the bathroom. He rested
his hands on the sink and fastened his eyes on his
reflection in the mirror. He sighed as he studied
himself, watching the troubled muscles move under the
skin, the eyes fragile, uncertain, remote and abstract,
like the eyes of a child determined not to cry. Returning
to the bedroom, he crossed over to the table and picked
up the small snapshot. The image of himself as a child
stared back at him, the hair bright ginger and eyes
brimming with joy. He crushed the photo, threw it in
the bin, headed towards the door, and went.

The sea slapped against the rocks, raging and frothing
and swirling and shelving up in spraying columns,
running away from the shore and softly over the dark
sands. Rupert scrambled up the cliff, managing to find
the correct footholds in the dark, grabbing at the
bracken for support, easing his weight from one ledge
to another. Upon reaching the arbor, he took a breath,
wiped the sweat from his brow, and retrieved the bottle
of whiskey from his coat pocket. It was cold and the
wind moved around him, tugging him this way and that.
He blinked and clutched tightly at the folds of his coat,
turning the bottle up and taking a long fortifying
swallow. He could discern the white crests of waves as
they broke on the shore below. The swift moving
clouds parted above him, and moonlight spilled for a
few seconds across the cliff, illuminating the surf as it

flowed back and along the beach. The sight of the moonlight mingled with his thoughts; memories appeared, steadily growing, ascending in his mind, taking on flesh, rising from the mists of childhood – he was a four-years-old again, standing on a lakefront dock. His parents were rowing a punt some distance away, quaffing wine and laughing. Numberless swans floated past as they rowed, the swans cleansing their feathers. Rupert made several attempts to join his parents, running close to the water and calling out to them, trying to draw their attention, but it was as if they couldn't hear him. His mother suddenly looked in his direction, noticing him standing on the dock on his own. There was a strange expression on her face. One that he had never seen before. She seemed cold in spite of the summers' day, for she shivered at the sight of him.

A strong wind blew in from the sea, almost pushing Rupert back into the arbor. He regained his footing, wrapped his overcoat around him tightly, and moved closer to the cliff-edge. The horizon was practically invisible now, distinguished from the sky only by the rumble of the waves. The wind howled, continuing to tug him this way and that, the waves rushing in his ears, mingling with the sound of his heart and blood. He imagined himself plummeting from the cliff, hanging in space for a few seconds, before hurtling down, watching the sea grow larger and larger. He hits the sea, tumbles and turns, flapping and hollering. The waves churn about him, the gravity pulls him down, plunging him into the black and crushing depths, down and down –down.

Ursula ran up the street as fast as her short legs could carry her, dodging in and out of the pedestrians, braless boobed and panting, her hair whipping back and forth as she ran. She rushed up Newborough Street, turned right onto St. Nicolas Street, passed the Grand hotel, and took the grueling ascent up the cliffs. On reaching the shelter, she started scanning the area, looking through the heather, gazing down at the rocks and chasms of bracken.

'Rupert!' she shouted, her eyes darting around, her powdered face strained with panic. 'Rupert! Rupert! *Rupert!*'

'I remember going to the coast as a child.'

She heard the voice behind her, and turned quickly. There, in the arbor, grey, pale, massive, but still handsome, sat Rupert, his rugged features cut in half by the slender wooden mullions that separated the windows.

'It was somewhere on the south coast,' he said. 'Near Eastbourne, I think. My mother and father were playing in the surf and were trying to get me to come in and join them. Have some fun, they kept on saying, loosen-up a bit. I did go in. I remember the waves, how they lapped against my legs, how the sand under my feet shifted with every step. I gave off a smile, I remember that –smiling, trying to show my parents that I was enjoying myself, that I was having fun. Suddenly a wave tumbled down from somewhere, pulling me under and grinding me against the pebbles. I churned around for what seemed ages, spinning and turning … helpless … out of control … like a piece of driftwood tossed about in the tide.' He paused, raised the bottle of whiskey and took a painful swallow. Then went on: 'I eventually came up, coughing out my guts, crawling along the sand, spitting away dirty water that had gathered in my mouth, and you know what I did – I laughed, yes … I *laughed*, even though I was a terrified out of my wits I laughed, trying to show my parents that I was having fun.' After a moments' hesitation in which he seemed to be collecting himself, he raised the whiskey and took another painful swallow, clenching his teeth at the burning. 'I was a lonely child,' he said, 'sensitive, inward looking, eager to please others. People called me the fairy child, the little sleepwalking boy, always walking around in circles and making funny noises to himself. When I went to London to read for the bar you could say my parents were pleased for me. They were two successful lawyers, did everything they could to get me in the place. The only thing was I wasn't cut out for the legal profession. In fact, it turned out I wasn't cut out for *any* profession.' He took another gulp of the whiskey, a barely perceptible expression of amusement on his face. 'To say my parents were disappointed is an understatement,' he said, 'I suppose when your son has the intellectual ability and ends up stacking shelves in a supermarket, it's heartbreaking.' He paused, his expression of amusement turning to puzzlement. He continued: 'I don't know what happened after that … I can't remember the details … a year ago … a month … last week … I was at home at the time … I'd just come back from one of my trips to the hospital. I woke one morning and everything became clear to me … everything became so very clear … so *clear*.' He raised his eyes and gazed at the black roaring sea. A cluster of lights had appeared on the horizon, a group of fishing boats heading out to shoot their nets under the cover of darkness. 'I knew what I must do after that,' he said, 'the only thing left worth doing. So, I packed up some things before my parents were awake and drove up here to Yorkshire … to find my lake … watch my last sunset on its banks … if I could find it that is –you helped me find it, Ursula. The only problem was I couldn't do it anymore.' He took another swallow of whiskey, polishing the bottle off and throwing it to the side of the arbor. He put his elbows on his knees and buried his face in his hands. A small paroxysm that was both half-giggle and half-sob shook him lightly. 'I couldn't do it!' he said. 'I couldn't do it! I couldn't do it to my parents! I couldn't do it to me! I couldn't do it to you! I couldn't do it to *life!*'

For a long moment neither of them spoke. The sound of the wind howled, the opera of the sea swelling beneath them. Rupert's head began to fall towards his chest. He was such a massive figure that it looked like as if it would be impossible for him ever to rise out of that small shelter. Ursula continued staring at him, lost at what to say. She noticed a long streak of a tear that had established itself under his eye. 'Look, Rupert' she said. 'You're alright. You just got lost along the way. We all get lost along the way once in a while. I mean look at me, the girl with chewing gum for brains an' wiggles her pink bits at weekends. Everyone has skeletons in their cupboards, some of us whole cemeteries. You're no different to anyone else.'

'I wish I could've been more like you, Ursula,' said Rupert, his voice straining. 'I wish I could've been the father you never had.'

'You're not my father, Rupert, you're *Rupert*, an aging, sweet, lonely man who drives a clapped-out old Porsche and doesn't know how to be himself. Be yourself, Rupert, everyone else is taken.'

Rupert passed a hand over his face. 'Where do I start?'
'You start at the beginning. You start each morning looking at yourself in the mirror and liking what you see, because that person is the only person that's going be your friend in life – you start with *you*!'
'I don't think I know how,' Rupert said.
'Yes, you do … c'mere' you silly twit.'
She put both hands out towards him. Rupert took the hands and stood out of the arbor. She slipped her hands out of his and felt his face, regarding his pale grey eyes and moist, unshaven cheeks. He looked ghostly in the cold darkness, and she saw the tears running like silver down his face. They left the arbor and started back to town. The downward slope of the cliff aided them as they went, and they began to trot.
'So how did you know I was up here?' Rupert asked as they trotted.
'I went to your hotel to look for you. The publican told me you'd gone for a walk along the south cliffs.'
'I went to see you tonight at the Queen Anne, but the bouncer on the door wouldn't let me in, thought I looked a bit dodgy.'
'Who, the incredible sulk? Don't worry 'bout him, us girls all think he's a twat-head. I don't think I'll work down the Queen Ann much longer if I'm honest; think I've outgrown the place –too many chavs. Say, Rupert d'ya fancy going over me Uncle Harry's for a cup o' brew? You'll like me Uncle Harry, he's a lot like you; deep thinker, likes spending time at home and in parks. Do you know he can solve the Rubik's Cube in twenty-point something seconds?'
'He sounds like a man after my own heart.'
'So anyroad, all this stuff you been telling me about being married, none of it's true?'
'No.'

'And you're not a lawyer.'

'Sorry.'

'What about the lake?'

'That's true … kind of.'

'Kind of?'

'I remember watching a film as a kid once where this boy discovers this enchanted lake in the forest.'

'Chuffin' eck! You telling me we've been chasing around North Yorkshire all because of some blinkin' film?'

'Not exactly, there *was* a lake, but I think it was a wedding reception outside Harrogate, some place with a beer garden and swans out the back.'

'Bloody-nora! You're a right one, you are, gate-crashing parties as a four-year-old. Say, Rupert, do you really think I have a favva complex?'

'Yes, I do.'

'I wouldn't mind, but I don't know what it means.'

Stage Door

It was a sunny afternoon in early November when Moses Peartree saw the flyer. It was just after three and he had been drinking since midday, ever since his mother had sent him out to get her a birthday card. There, near the pub entrance of Dirty Dick's in Bishopsgate was a table full of flyers of the latest West End plays. The most conspicuous one showed a picture of a woman wearing a wide-brimmed brown felt hat at an angle, with fresh yellow flowers pinned to the band. She was smiling, one of those subtle smiles, visible as though under the skin. Forcing down the remainder of his beer, Moses walked over to the flyer and picked it up.

Tessa Jefford   Alan Rogers

Last Tango in Paris

By
Richard Richards
12 WEEKS ONLY. COMEDY THEATRE

He couldn't believe it. It was *her*. How long had it
been? Ten? Fifteen years? No, more. How oddly remote
it seemed to him now, and irrelevant, like something
seen through the wrong end of a telescope. He'd grown
up in that time, grown out of that type of thing, like a
child grows out of clothes, grown bigger and the clothes
become too small. Or so he thought. He stared at the
flyer, his brow creased and face tensed, eyes fixed as if
staring at something a yard behind his head. For a
moment he was lost in a transitory evocation of the
past. He remembered standing in the newsagents at the
end of his road, musing on whether to buy Dolly
Mixtures or Mint Imperials as he flipped through a
copy of the *TVTimes*. There, above a half-page spread
of the Two Ronnies was an advertisement for some new
American TV series. The featured article displayed a
picture of a young woman bathing in a pool. Her hair
was light, reddish-brown, and she wore it piled in thick
tresses upon her head. She had a precisely shaped
mouth, and wore an ornate crystal necklace which
covered her neck and part of her breasts. But it was the
eyes which caught Moses. They were an arctic blue,
almost white, with flecks of silvery ice. There was
something about those eyes, something ageless, not a
child, not an adult. A sincere almost sad longing.
Moses had been captivated by the image and had asked
people who the woman was. Everybody seemed to
know. It was Tessa Jefford from the hit sci-fi series
Private Investigators in Space. Ever since its pilot at
Christmas, the series had been a howling success,
settling almost immediately into a comfortable Friday
night habit for the science fiction enthusiasts. Set in the
year 2085, the series focused on a secret operative on a
classified mission, a clandestine aeronautical operation
that reached beyond the bounds of the possible to make

the most momentous journey since Armstrong had landed on the moon. The supporting female character – Tessa Jefford – was a fortune-teller who assisted the lead male role in foiling the plots of extra-terrestrials and other interdimensional beings who inhabited the red dwarfs and multiplanetary systems of Alpha Centauri, including several species of sandworm on the worlds of Gama Andromeda and Europa. Even though he thought the series somewhat of a let-down, and some of the scenes rather cringeworthy, Moses ended up buying season 1 on VHS box-set, including other subsequent seasons over the next few years. He covered his walls with cut-out pictures of the actress Tessa Jefford, plastering every available space in his bedroom. There was Tessa Jefford in government-issued power suits and wire-rimmed glasses, Tessa Jefford in black lace nightwear lying on a caribou rug in front of a raging fire in Canada, Tessa Jefford in a plunging neckline with her ass hanging out and hair blow-dried to within an inch of her life at some Los Angeles gala ball, Tessa Jefford in a hat plume and bodice reclining in a brothel in turn-of-the-century Paris, Tessa Jefford in silver wellingtons and formfitting jumpsuit wrapped in clingfilm whilst holding a laser pistol and being mounted from behind by a four-foot black-eyed alien –Moses' bedroom was a veritable shrine to the actress. He found out everything he could about her, checking out biographies, interviews, filming anecdotes. He followed her latest dresses in girls' magazines and fashion periodicals to learn where she got her inspiration for her clothing. He chartered her achingly trendy behind-the-scenes fashion shoots; pictures of dogs and videos of her trying to spin a basketball on one finger.

Born into a dysfunctional family in Pocahontas, Virginia, Tessa Marie Jefford had enrolled at the Minnesota State University Drama School, gaining a Bachelor of Fine Arts Degree and setting off to New York to seek stardom. She spent several years in New York, settling into the lifestyle of the struggling actress, going on numerous auditions for off-Broadway and experimental, fringe productions and failing to get the parts. After appearing in a production of *The Taming of the Shrew* at the Long Wharf Theatre in New Haven, Connecticut, she found herself compromising her professional integrity and buying a ticket to LA. Unfortunately, over the next two years her East Coast reputation only translated to yet another out-of-work actress on the streets of Hollywood. At some point her agent rung her about an audition for a new pilot episode called *Private Investigators in Space*. The casting for the show had been long and arduous, but Tessa had eventually got the part. By the summer of the same year *Private Investigators in Space* was no longer a cult pilot show but was making major strides into mainstream television, progressing in the second season from big hit to critical ratings top dog and graduating to full-blown *Star Trek* level pop culture phenomenon. By season three Jefford was an A-lister, or near to. She ended up marrying the assistant art director on the show after falling pregnant. Their son 'Berlin' was born shortly after, though by the following year the couple divorced, the husband claiming that Tessa had had extra marital relations during their marriage. By Christmas of the same year Jefford was pregnant again, the father this time being Dirk Doggone, founding member of the funk rock group, the *Matrix Headcases,* marrying him just three days after divorcing her first husband. Unfortunately, the relationship wouldn't last as long as the pregnancy, with the couple separating three months later. In August of 1987, a controversy arose when a low-budget TV film appeared showing Tessa in a semi-nude act. Released during the peak of the *Private Investigators* popularity, the video cover displayed a single shot of Tessa Jefford pulling down a lacy bodice, exposing two small pert breasts as she gazed demurely into the camera. The film, which was set during the American Civil War, saw Tessa playing a southern belle –something everyone was confident she could do due to her Virginian upbringing –and involved a marauding Yankee cavalry soldier bursting into her room, brandishing a pistol, and ravishing her voraciously. After the film was bought by some British film distributor, it had instantly been released on home video. On which Tessa had hired lawyers in an attempt to stop the films' release. The British tabloids described the film as a 'B-movie,' claiming that Tessa had tried to buy back the film for large sums of money, without success. Tessa had apparently had a clause in her contract when she had made the film, stating that her breasts should not be exposed in any of the scenes. Despite the controversy, the judge said the scene was 'fleeting' and didn't deserve the attention it spawned. The film, in fact, was amateurish, the famous breasts occupying less than ten seconds of screen time, although it did, for a while, enjoy a certain vogue amongst the smart fetishist set, the so-called 'Boots and Period' crowd.

By September 1989, Moses' obsession with Tessa Jefford was starting to wane, and he lost himself in other pursuits, such as early modern European history and lesbian porn. When he was older, he would look back upon this episode in his life as if it were an unreal time that belonged to someone else, a time that had passed not in the regular flow to which he was accustomed, but an intensive idyllic and rather disturbing reverie. His parents, admittedly, were relieved when he took down the posters of the actress, deciding instead to put up a thousand-piece jigsaw puzzle of the Mona Lisa and a life-size picture of Sylvester Stallone in *Rambo: First Blood Part II*.

☐

He couldn't believe it. Tessa Jefford, his teenage calendar crush, was in London. The play was set to start in a weeks' time, and Moses got the nearest available ticket to that for the Sunday, the ticket to be collected at the box office on the night of the performance. Tessa had been in London exactly two weeks, and rehearsals had progressed at an accelerated pace. Her arrival had not been without certain fanfare, mainly due to her agent leaking it, rather profusely, to all the media outlets, so that she would get as much publicity on touch down as possible. Moses found out what he could about the play before, buying the daily newspapers and listing magazines. There was a substantial side article on page three of the *Evening Standard's* free entertainment supplement, which showed Tessa lying naked on a mattress with her male co-star, the bed covers pooled around their waists as they gazed pensively into the camera.
The article read:

With the recent influx of Hollywood stars into the London theatre, Tessa Jefford of *Private Investigators in Space* fame is to join the ranks of American actors treading the boards of the West End. As the sci-fi geeks preferred pinup of the 1980s, she was a global star at the age of nineteen. But, after twenty years of being in the shadow of the hit television series, she has been aching to return to her roots in theatre. And what better way to do it than a debut performance in a two-hander in the West End. One of the great erotic films of the 1970s, *Last Tango in Paris* tells the story of a middle-aged American man who takes up an anonymous sexual relationship with a young French woman in an apartment in Paris. Tessa Jefford is to play the part of Maria Scheider's, Jeanne, and the British actor Alan Rogers (fresh from his performance in Pinter's *The Caretaker* at the Old Vic), the part of Marlon Brando's, Paul. It's adaption for the stage is by a new American writer, Richard Richards. To date, the demand on Jefford's acting ability had been negligible, and that would include the parts she has played off Broadway. Her acting talent has never really been tested. None of her appearances in front of the camera have required more than energetic movements and displays of poutiness. *Last Tango* will be the first time she has had to create a full character and be an equal member of an ensemble company. 'Forgetting my lines is my worst nightmare,' she told us over cold duck and orange *pâté* in a Notting Hill restaurant, 'but I have worked out with the director a few coping strategies if anything goes wrong.' The speculation from the press about the play has so far been amiable, although certain critics have already started expressing their reservations, saying that Jefford is playing a character twenty years younger than she actually is, and that the play is too controversial due to its subject matter centring around a submissive younger woman being brutalized by a dominant older man. Tessa rebuked these accusations in our interview, stating that the character she is playing is a strong independent woman, and that she would never allow herself to be involved in any oppressive portrayal of her gender. She went on to say that the play is more about loneliness and anguish than it is about sex. She even suggested that it would have been more courageous for the director to have re-moulded the play for a modern audience and have Jeanne make it with an older woman. The play is set to open in November and have a twelve-week run at the Comedy Theatre in Panton Street, Haymarket.

Apart from the *Evening Standard's* article, the other tabloids hardly touched on the play. The *Guardian* had a short piece discussing how Tessa was enjoying being in London, whilst Tuesdays' *Metro* showed the cast going through one of its final run-throughs, the picture unfolding showing Paul throwing himself at the young, compliant Jeanne. The only other comprehensive article was found in *FHM* –the magazine that had once voted Tessa Jefford the sexiest women alive –which had a full photospread of Tessa reclining on a penthouse sofa, followed by an intimate interview on the inside pages. It read:

For ten years she has lived in a world populated by aliens, interdimensional beings, and blubbery jelly-type creatures that wanted to suck her face off. Now, at the age of 42, Tessa Jefford is trying her hand at the London theatre in a stage adaptation of Bernardo Bertolucci's infamous film, *Last Tango in Paris.* We met up with her for lunch at the Savoy, where she has spent three days prior to rehearsals doing scattered press interviews and, rumour has it, seeing a young London-based film-editor she met at Cannes. Jefford has a peculiar charm about her, a certain winsomeness mixed with an undercurrent of rigidity, with occasional outbursts of infectious mirth. She speaks fluidly and elegantly in an accent somewhere between refined English and soft American, a transatlantic fad she has picked up from her life-long friend, the pop star – Magdalen. Since divorcing her sixth husband – the South African photojournalist and documentary filmmaker, Dee Richmond-Cowen –Jefford has been a lot happier in her life; jogging four times a week, eating frozen yoghourt for breakfast, and getting into a fitness regime which involves a mixture of resistance training and some new phenomenon called Chocolate Yoga – I Ching with Ferrero Rocher. Her marriage to Richmond-Cowen lasted just eight months, the divorce papers citing 'unreasonable behaviour' for their separation. Stories had circulated that their marriage had been on the rocks after a supposed bizarre alcohol-fueled outburst by Jefford on a flight from New York to Swaziland. The stories claimed that Richmond-Cowen was not getting on with Jefford's son from her first marriage –'Berlin.' Other sources claimed that they were having 'irreconcilable marital differences', and as such, had decided to mutually call it a day. 'I've had a blessed life,' she said to us over a glass of Pinot and platter of smoked salmon. 'I don't see the end of my relationships as a failure. Certainly, the times I've had with any of the partners have been majoritively joyful and pleasant, and I have some beautiful children to show for it.' On getting the part in *Last Tango* she told us she couldn't have been more delighted. In Los Angeles, on the morning she reccived the call from the director that they wanted her for the part, the first thing she had done was rush over to the actors' workshop in Santa Monica and tell her guru – the renowned Reverend Mother Anastasia Yastbranovich – the wonderful news. She kept on emphasising during our interview how great it was to have been given the opportunity to do other work now she wasn't under contract to the studios, and that the play was in many ways what she had been working towards her whole career; to do, as she said, 'something creative,' something which, 'pushed her emotionally.' The part has apparently come as a relief to Jefford. Although one of the highest-paid TV stars in the 80s, she has remained completely unproven as an actress. '*Last Tango* will be a totally new experience for me,' she said to us, the enthusiasm in her voice becoming more real, 'for the first time I will be required to do something that doesn't come easily. It will mean work and concentration, but clearly the effort in personal, if not in public, will be worth it in the end.' We hope so for your sake Tessa. After all, anything's got to be better than spending your time attending sci-fi conventions, having walk-on cameos on daytime television, and reading several thousand fan letters each week, mostly from nostalgic thirty-something sci-fi nerds and the occasional sex-nut.

□

The night of the performance came around. Moses dressed up for the occasion. Tie, pressed trousers, jacket, polished shoes. His parents had never seen him look so smart. He got the early train into London, having a drink at the bar in the Royal festival Hal, and spending a few hours browsing the book shops in Charing Cross Road. He was used to walking the roads of London, wandering the back roads, this way and that. He would move through the streets of bodies from early evening till late. The people would flow around him in a collective mass, like they were part of some mysterious coordinated activity, to which only he, Moses Peartree, stood apart, alone and disaffected. Sometimes he would see people walking towards him, in his general direction, but they never seemed to reach him, turning left or turning right or disappearing altogether. He would listen to a million words and peer into a hundred thousand faces –secret, dark, unknown, nameless faces – and although he did not speak to the people, he would sometimes feel a kinship with them, a sense of belonging, a fellow atom in the swarming streets of life. Occasionally, as a kind of relief from the crowds, he would sit in St. Patrick's Catholic Church in Soho Square. He would sit there for an hour, his hands clutching themselves, staring around the old church, gazing at the massive gold of the altar-piece, the sumptuous iron-work, gilt and faded, the air laden with incense. He would allow his mind to wander, feeling that sense, that undeniable brevity of presence, the *sacredness,* then, as if waking from a dream, he would rise from the pew and walk back down the nave and out the door, leaving the sacredness behind and moving again amongst the entertainment venues, the pubs, sex shops, market stalls –a solitary silhouette against the city glow.

Moses Malabranca Peartree –his middle name inspired by the sequence *Dies irae* in Mozart's Requiem, due to his parents conceiving him on the night of a celebrated performance in St. Martin-in-the-Fields in the summer of 1969 –was a tall man of middle weight and slight form. His nails were bitten to the quick, and his hands were small-boned, fleshless as a claw, with pale grey eyes and a cow's lick of thick brown hair brushed over his head like a birds' nest. He was a good-looking young man, though too tall for his build, were he a few inches shorter he would have been more handsome, for it was as if he stopped growing only to be stretched on one of those medieval racks a half-foot more. He would always wear the same cheap make jeans, with some sort of red, green or yellow checkered shirt, summer or winter, his thin wrists protruding from the sleeves of the shirt, the jeans riding awkwardly about the legs, as if they were clothes that had belonged to a younger version of himself. He possessed an introverted outlook, was intense and awkward, a slow starter in the conversations, not saying much and prone to bouts of silence, and when he did speak, he seemed to speak too quickly, like he would never have enough time fully to explain his point, his small-boned hands moving restlessly as if over-compensating by adding too much to the conversation. His introversion was the reason why he was often found alone, preferring to pursue his own lonely way in life. This secretiveness was not, however, incompatible with powerful emotions. He passionately loved films, books, painting; he was deeply attached to his home and to his bedroom and his dog and garden. Violent impulses, gusts of consuming passions not only of love, but of hatred and anger too, were an important element of his private world; but they existed even in childhood behind a high wall of self-repression. He only let himself go in situations where other people were not immediately and personally involved. He could be ardently enthusiastic about particular ideas and beliefs, but shrank from what he felt to be the indecency of expressed emotional intimacy with others.

At thirty-two he was still living at home with his parents, spending most of his days in his bedroom and nights walking the streets of London. He seldom ate dinner with his parents now he was older, but he would eat whatever his mother put before him –preferring to eat meat and pink blancmange, and often ate the dessert first. At weekends he would watch television with his parents, sometimes a comedy show, but the bursts of laughter from the studio audience bothered Moses for he had no sense of humor. His bedroom comprised of an unmade bed, a stack of theological periodicals, a row of second-hand paperbacks, some loose piles of print-outs, a table with several half-drunk coffee mugs, a bureau with an ornament of a Roman helmet; some pieces of clothing, a dictionary, a whicker linen basket, an empty cardboard box –his book. It was moving to think that his book is, *was*, his great unfinished task. He would often imagine the cardboard box crammed with notes, doggerels, dairies, scribbling's, half-formed thoughts, inspirational moments, remembered anecdotes. There would be pieces of paper studded with quotations and aphorisms, new ideas written in margins, coffee rings over paragraphs. There would be drafting's, redrafting's, rewriting's, reimagining's, tinkering's, revisions, a nip and tuck here, a cut there, an addition over there, reshuffling imperfections of initial attempts, sentences that were once judged complete crying out for re-composition or elaboration and development with some new idea, image, or metaphor. He would imagine the box filled with a multitudinous collection of stories from the past and the future, a vast rambling compendium of tales, allegories, and parables, quotations, narrations, citations. It would be a philosophical credo, though by no means be exhaustible, moving from essay format to first-person narrative and back to essay almost seamlessly. It would be a diary, a dreamjournal, a dialectic, a self-exploration, a cathartic confession, maybe sounding in

111

places officious, maybe sardonic, or perhaps pretentious, portraying the author as a polymath or an essayist, slightly pontifical and a touch disillusioned, or perhaps avowedly pedantic. At times Moses wanted the book to be a gratuitous work, for private consumption, to be read only by friends and the immediate family. He would fantasise distant relatives stumbling across it in a hundred years –hidden away in some dusty attic for remote posterity to read and ponder, maybe even shed a few tears over. He thought all these things, but in point of fact, he had never written a word of it. Maybe he was too afraid to. Maybe he felt like it was an impossible task to complete. There was just too much to say, it was beyond him. He used to often fret over that book, like he had to scribble down everything right there just in case he forgot the feeling or whatever, but something always stopped him from doing it. He didn't really think about it that much anymore. He guessed he couldn't be bothered because it seemed too scary, but mostly it seemed ridiculous. So now he just had this empty cardboard box in his bedroom, this stupid carboard box which had *'book'* written on the front as he awaited the muse to overtake him, which it never did.

The Comedy Theatre was a small theatre near Piccadilly Circus, the façade one of painted stucco and brick. It was one of the more elegant theatres in the West End, a flamboyant Victorian structure with intricate mouldings and an elaborate cast-iron canopy. To stare at it one wouldn't have thought it belonged to the harsh, contemporary world surrounding it. Car

112

horns could not be construed as its music, the blueness of the sky was too pure and too abrupt. It was like witnessing a ghost, a faded sophistication of a world no longer in existence, like a mausoleum, grand in concept and construction, whose workers and actors could never be equated to its majesty and had allowed it to go into decline.

Moses stood on the steps of the Comedy Theatre, staring through its double glass doors at a collection of people in evening attire, conversing with each other in a mixture of excitement and irritation as the bar staff scuttled around them with trays of brimming glasses. His eyes wandered to the marquee above the doors, the image on it showing the picture from the flyer in Dirty Dick's: Tessa in a wide-brimmed felt hat, with fresh flowers pinned to the band –no hint of the male actor. Under the marquee several signs hung by chains from the canopy, saying:

MAGNIFICENT

and:

HUGELY ENTERTAINING

and:

A MUST-SEE SULTRY EXAMINATION OF LOVE AND PERSONAL OBSESSION

and:

A TOUR DE FORCE ÉROTICA, UNIQUE IN THE HISTORY OF CONTEMPORARY THEATRE

Moses wiped his mouth on his sleeve and moved respectfully –fearfully –up the steps of the theatre and into the foyer. He collected his ticket at the box office and went to get a drink at the bar. He ordered a medium dry white wine and backed into one of the corridors leading to the auditorium. It was press night, and there was a host of critics, reviewers, bloggers, and lower-middle celebrities around. The feeling was intense, disturbing –enthralling. It gave Moses a delightful sense of being with great and celebrated people, people who were experts in the subtlest processes of social etiquette; well-travelled, urbane, sophisticated and assured, telling jovial anecdotes about famous figures they had known and on whom were on such familiar terms –told always apropos of some topic of discussion casually, never dragged in or laboured by pretence.

The bell rang, indicating that the play was about to start. People finished their drinks and made their way into the auditorium, the ushers directing them to their seats, shepherding them like souls to the underworld. The lights dimmed, and the people settled down. The curtain raised. A man could be seen sitting on a radiator beside the door to an apartment, partly in shadow. The door to the apartment opened and a woman made her way in. She crossed to the window and opened the shutters, gazing out at a painted backdrop of Paris – Tessa Jefford. She turned and started moving around the apartment, swinging her handbag on its leather thong, her hips moving from side to side, her white suede coat half-open, revealing a yellow thigh-length skirt and tighted legs, most of them lost in the embrace of soft, calfskin boots.

She stopped when she noticed the man on the radiator. '*Qui êtes vous?*' she asked, biting her fist in fright, to which, walking slowly into the light, with seventies

sideburns and a mocking expression, came the actor
Alan Rogers. He swept Tessa up in his arms, pushed
her against the wall, wrenched open his trousers, and,
grasping buttocks in both hands, pretended to fuck her.
The audience gasped. Moses sank back in his seat. Alan
Rogers applied himself once more to Tessa, lips and
tongue, with renewed zeal, placing his hands more
firmly under her buttocks. Tessa sighed, moaned,
panted, opened her mouth, and with shuddering body
let out a resounding wail –*Ung, ung, ung, ung, uuuuuuu
uuuuuuuungaaaaaaaaaaaaaaaaaaaaaaaaaaaaaaaaaaaaa
aaahhhh!*
With a great gasp and a sob, she pulled away from his
thrusting body and fell to the ground, lying on the floor
and staring at the audience, her delicately flowered,
girlishly innocent and slightly torn, clothing entwined
with the crude outer garments of Rogers. The audience
looked on in suspended silence, too stunned to move, to
even breathe, frozen in a paralysis of horrified
fascination.
'*Mon Dieu!*' said Tessa. '*Mon Dieu! Oh, la...la.*'

□

'I don't know who he is … I don't know him … he
tried to rape me … I don't know who he is … he's a
madman!' Tessa stood on the balcony of the apartment,
a smoking gun in her hand, the body of Rogers lying in
a foetal position at her feet, curled up like a child in
sleep. 'I don't know who he is,' she repeated. 'I don't
know him … he wanted to rape me … I don't know his
name … he was crazy … I don't …'
There was a hushed silence. The curtain fell. The lights
faded. The audience started clapping, were brought to

their feet more than once. The applause was loud and respectful. The auditorium cheered, called out, clapped, whistled. Tessa came back on stage for an encore. She stood acknowledging the applause, soaking up the accolades, smiling as much as humility allowed. A girl, holding a bouquet of flowers, deposited her offerings on the stage at Tessa's feet. Tessa took the flowers and, throwing a kiss to someone in the balcony, exited. The applause subsided, and people went to leave. The crowd filed out of the theatre. The fans for the most departed, except for a handful of diehards who remained, gathering under some scaffolding at the side of the theatre. There, obscured by the scaffolding, was the stage door. Moses joined the queue under the scaffolding, standing anxious, chewing his nails, wringing his hands, shifting uncomfortably from foot to foot as he listened to the banter of the people in the queue.

'Didn't her hair look nice –very seventies I'd say.'
'Yes, they say she had her perm done quite early for it.'
'Yes, that's right. Some stylist in Covent Garden, I heard.'

'She's much prettier in real life than she looks on TV, doesn't she. I mean, she looks nice on TV, but she looks fan*tast*ic in real life.'
'My sentiments exactly. And no spring chicken either.'

'Personally, I always admired her for her naturalness. She's not fake and plastic like other actresses in Hollywood. She never cared that people always criticized the size of her nose. She never changed her looks to please others. And why should she? She's perfect the way she is.'

'Yes, she's certainly something that Tessa Jefford. Did you see that look in her eyes as he was shoving the butter up her crack? It was so vulnerable. So heart-rending. But that's Tessa Jefford for you. Always the pro, always emotionally available for whatever is called for.'

'Look! There she is! Tessa! Tessa, we love you! Tessa! Tessa! Over here!'

A roar came from the crowd as Tessa emerged at the stage door. She gave a greeting to the waiting fans, smiled– suggestive that the level of hysteria was not new to her – and, felt-tip pen in hand, reached out to receive their programmes. The queue started moving quickly, decreasing rapidly, as the people exchanged small tête-à-têtes with Tessa and moved on. Before he knew it, Moses was just two people away from Tessa. His nerves were still shooting off inside him. He swallowed, patted his hair down, rubbed it back around the sides, stuck out his hand and said: 'Hello.'
'Hello,' said Tessa.
'It's good to meet you. I was – *am*, one of your biggest fans. I used to have pictures of you all over my walls when I was a kid. I even had pictures of you on the ceiling above my bed.' His cheeks reddened at the comment.
'Did you feel like you had to say that?' Tessa said, a trace of irritation insinuated into her voice.
'I suppose,' Moses admitted. His colour deepened.
'Well, it was nice meeting you at last.'
She forced a smile.
Moses nodded and moved on, scampering away as two excitable girls came up with their handful of

117

nauseatingly glossy fan fiction. After five minutes the queue dispersed. Tessa signed the last few remaining items, gave some perfunctory quotes to some reporters, and headed for a waiting limo at the curb. 'We love you, Tessa!' the fans shouted as she stepped into the limo, which pulled out and headed up the street, disappearing into the traffic of the West End. Clutching his recently autographed flyer, Moses crossed the road and entered the pub opposite the theatre. He stood at the bar, cradling a scotch and ice, his cheeks flushed, eyes blinking, a silly grin plastered across his face. It hadn't gone too bad, he thought. Not too bad at all. He had tried to look and sound casual; normal anyway –casual was beyond him. But it hadn't gone too bad. In a sense, it didn't matter how it had gone. He had finally done it; spoken to his teenage pinup, the woman that his acned star-struck seventeen-year old self had discharged copious amounts of bodily fluid over. It felt surreal seeing her in person after ogling her from cut-out pictures for so many years. Seeing her in the flesh had certainly been an experience. She had been shorter than he expected, her skin not as perfect as he thought. But she had looked so much more real in person, so much more human. He left the pub just as it was busying. He could've gone down the next pub up the street –it was only a few minutes' walk –but he didn't bother, deciding to get a Big Mac and fries in Leicester Square and the next train home, which he did.

▢

Moses woke the following day feeling flat and disaffected. He went down the shops and bought the morning papers, combing them for the reviews of the play. The *Observer* regarded it as 'thinner in texture,' than the film version; the *Guardian* describing the play as essentially 'untheatrical,' and Paul's '… metaphor as over-extended.' For the *Independent* the entire evening proved to be a colossal bore, whereas an anonymous *Times* drama critic expressed grave reservations for Tessa's performance, finding that the demands of the French dialect defeated her, and that the miscast of her as a young woman was more distracting than immersing. In so many words, the play had panned. The only kind words were to be found in the *Daily Mirror,* which said Tessa's performance was 'moderately perceptive,' and that '…every gesture has a kind of contained sexual drive.' The most scathing review was found in the *Sunday Telegraph,* which ran with a half-page article. It read:

PRIVATE INVESTIGATORS IN SPACE PLAY FAILS TO IMPRESS!

The list of Hollywood actors and actresses crossing the pond to appear in the West End smacks of attempting to add credibility to their CV –but Tessa Jefford hardly gives a career-defining performance in her debut performance. From the very moment the curtain rises, we know that Jefford and Rogers are going to take carnal occupation of each other, and very soon. This we have all been eagerly anticipating since Jefford's announcement back in the summer that she was going to appear on the London stage in an adaptation of Bertolucci's erotic film, *Last Tango in Paris*. The play starts immediately in the empty apartment, cutting out the opening sequence on the *Pont de Bir-Hakeim* for practical purposes. Abruptly, Rogers cashes the cheque

Brando did for us thirty years ago –he screws the heroine standing upright, or appears to, as we see no nudity or casting aside of garments, just simulated sex for an audience that feels like it has been short-changed out of its peephole experience. This is a sanitized version of the film. There is no greasing the ass with butter before the commencement of buggery. There is no dangling of dead rats with offerings to eat it with lashings of mayonnaise. There is no powerful erotic moment here. Jefford doesn't seem to have the screen presence of Maria Schneider, Rogers isn't a sexual heavyweight like Brando. Jefford's performance is at best wooden, so quiet that, at times, it is almost hard to hear, even when she is being taken from behind with low-cal olive spread –a mark down from the full-fat butter of the 70s I might add. Rogers admittedly seems more at ease in his role, who, despite an uncomfortable American accent, holds his more serious character (the only character he seems to be offered nowadays: the older man –solitary, cold – but with an undercurrent of repressed sensuality) – and provides a much-needed contrast to Jefford's 'supposed' adolescent Jeanne. For all its attempts at shock and titillation, the play version of *Last Tango in Paris* is an unreserved disappointment. More dry-humping than sloppy butter seconds.

Regardless of what the tabloids said, Moses Peartree hadn't minded the play. Tessa had seemed quite adorable as the twenty-year-old Jeanne. Perhaps it wasn't ground breaking theatre, but from what he knew very few shows could claim that. There had been a small point when Tessa had nearly floundered her lines –the scene in the tub where Rogers is scrubbing her feet –but apart from that he thought it was as good a piece of theatre as any, not that that he had seen a lot of theatre.

The week passed and Moses continued thinking about Tessa and his meeting with her. It hadn't gone brilliantly, he knew that, although, he fancied she'd given him a curious look when he had spoken to her. He was unable to interpret the exact meaning of that look, but it suggested to his mind the possibility of her in some way liking him and what he had said, and no sooner had the idea arisen with its enormous potentialities that it formulated as a secret practical ambition, a solid reality, to confirm such a liking. He must see her again and put his theory to the test. He went into London the following Saturday, his hair neatly trimmed and wearing his new coat his parents had just bought him for his birthday –a brown corduroy waist-length jacket, with flap pockets, two piped pockets on the side and back, and a white fur collar. Moses wasn't crazy about the coat, thought it made him look like a pimp, and it hung a bit loosely around the waist. But it was December and getting cold and his parents didn't want him to catch his death.

He got the train into London and went over to see his grandmother in Wandsworth, then got the train into Waterloo and walked over to the West End. It was a seeping, sluggish night in London's theatre district. Rain drifted idly through the sky. Taxi's and umbrellas congested everywhere you looked, and thick black clouds hung threateningly over the BT Tower. Moses surveyed a row of eateries opposite the Hippodrome in Leicester Square. But he wasn't hungry, and decided on a drink in the pub across the street from the Comedy Theatre. He went up to the bar and ordered a scotch and ice, sipping the drink in small, fast amounts as he stared at his reflection in the mirror behind the bar. He fidgeted in his new coat, giving it a nip and tuck around the back, a pull and pinch at the sides. He tried to make a long dent in the waist, in vain. It filled out immediately, similar to how a punctured ball won't retain an impression. Irritated, he finished his scotch and left the pub. A crowd had already gathered at the stage door, neatly formed under the scaffolding. After several minutes Tessa materialized at the door. She gave a brief greeting to the people and started signing their programmes. Moses joined the queue, standing in line as he had the previous week, shuffling from foot to foot, feeling tight, apprehensive, fighting away an instinct to retreat. It came to his turn.

'Hi,' he said, and Tessa answered, 'Hi.'

'You know, I met you last week.'

'Really.'

'Yes, a week ago. I don't know what it was, I just felt I wanted to see you again. I suppose that's sad really … I mean it's sad really, isn't it?'

'If you say it is.'

'Yes, I think it is. Anyway –don't mind me for asking – but does this coat look big on me?'

'I'm sorry?'

'My coat, does it look big on me?'

'It looks okay.'

'It's just that my parents bought it for me for my birthday and I'm not sure about it. I mean it's not too loose around the waist, is it? A bit loose, I think. How do you think it looks?'

'It looks fine.'

'Alright, I'll take your word for it. Well, it was nice meeting you again Tessa – Goodbye.'

He shook her hand, and left quickly, manoeuvring his way back through the crowd, jostling through the bodies and thrusting himself onto the road; he turned on the road and stared back at Tessa. There was a slight opening in the crowd, and she was standing there. She was staring at him, the expression on her face one of genuine, if not wan amusement. Then she did something strange, as shocking to Moses as if she had thrown off her clothes –she smiled at him. Moses returned the smile, turned, and walked promptly away up the street. He walked around for several hours. It was busy and still raining heavily in London. Tail lights gave out red reflections on the wet roads. Late shoppers and pedestrians pressed along the pavements; the buses disgorged the crowds. By the time he got home Moses was drenched, his bouncy hair slicked flat against his skull, but he didn't care. He went up to his bedroom without speaking to anyone, took off his damp clothes, put on his paisley pyjamas, and slipped between the sheets. He tried to sleep, but he couldn't, really didn't want to. He kept thinking about Tessa and the way she had smiled at him. That *smile*. It was brief, fleeting – a quick exchange, the keeping of eye contact, then the look quickly away before looking quickly back again. Moses knew that smile, even though he had never seen it before he knew it. All men knew it. It was the look of approval, an indication of interest in a way that was more than mere friendliness, more than a display of affection for a celebrities' adoring audience. And something else had happened. His voice had seemed to have energy behind it when he had spoken to her. He had expected a squeak to come out, something akin to the sound of a new-born kitten, but instead the words had flowed from his mouth, practically fall from his lips, as if they had been sitting there in his head for a long time. It wasn't so much what he had said as the way he had said it. Who cared about an oversized brown corduroy jacket with engraved snap buttons? It had been the tone of his voice, mixed with what he imagined was a reassuringly cheeky grin. He stretched himself out on his bed like a dog, smiling broadly, sighing deeply, feeling happier and happier. He couldn't remember ever feeling so happy. In fact, if anyone had asked him, and he had to answer honestly, looking back, he would have said it was the happiest, the very best, moment of his life.

☐

Morning chased away the storm. The clouds receded rapidly, vaporizing as if they had never been. Moses spent the entire day thinking about Tessa Jefford and his meeting with her. He couldn't stop thinking about how she had smiled at him; the way her face had been so alive, so animated. It was like her eyes were lit from the inside, those large round arctic-blue irises piercing through the rain and crowd towards him like a lance. Maybe she always reacted to fans in such a personable and friendly manner. Maybe she had sensed his genuine adoration of her. But he couldn't get that smile out of his head. She had smiled at him, smiled at *him,* not someone else. Him! He didn't feel she would have smiled at someone like that under normal circumstances. She had *noticed* him. But had she? Could he really be sure of that? After all, it had only been a smile, a nice one yes, but still only that –a smile. Why would that smile be different from any other smile she gave to any other person, if not millions of people she had smiled at over the years. And why would she give it to him: Moses Peartree, the outcast, the nobody. For the rest of the week he tried to put the meeting with Tessa Jefford out of his head, occupying himself with things like watching films or reading books, but it was hopeless. He would go over and over the encounter with Tessa Jefford, remembering the way she had smiled, the way she had looked. There was no way he could convey the intensity of how that smile made him feel. Only someone who had had a similar experience could possibly appreciate what he felt and still felt. It was as if that rainy night, for reasons he couldn't comprehend, Tessa and himself had slipped outside of reality, as if they had inhabited for those few brief seconds their own intimate dimension, a gap in time specifically made for them, as if the universe had conspired to create the moment just for them. The recollection of the event remained with him, like an incorporated form, but more substantial than a shadow, and the sight continually distracted his attention. He would pace up and down his room, or pause dreaming by the window, carrying on in his head the meeting. He would lie awake in the early hours of the morning, in a strange comatose state of joy and exhilaration, his eyes wide, wide and awake, plucking at the bogies in the cleft of his nostril as he made up various scenarios in his head, some of them ridiculous. At one moment he would be laughing with Tessa at the stage door about something or other. At another she was laughing at his jokes and slipping him her number. At another he was some kind of famous journalist who had been invited back to her hotel for an exclusive. They would share humorous conversations over champagne and truffles, that sparkle in her eyes growing ever larger, the chatter going on and on through the night, asking about each other's lives.

'*So, where did you get that coat anyway?*'
'*Do you like it?*'
'*Very much.*'

'It looks so well on you.'
'Why thank you.'
'Not at all. How is your book going?'
'I'm still gathering material for it; you can read what I've written so far.'
'I shall like that.'
'Come out with me tonight.'
'What?'
'I said come out with me tonight.'
'Where?'
'Anywhere, for a walk, maybe through Soho in the rain.'
'I don't want to walk.'
'Then a pub, perhaps. I know this lovely little place just around the corner from the Comedy Theatre. What do you say?'

He would weave new and more preposterous fables. He was swept along in the full tide of his adventure; he thought of nothing else. It was as if his whole being, his soul, his mind and body, were centralized on Tessa Jefford, like his whole life relied upon, and was dependent upon that smile. Without that smile he was nothing, just a lifeless body, a machine going through the motions. In the afternoons he had to almost physically restrain himself from rising from his bed, hurrying out the door and getting the train into London. In the end there was nothing else he could do. No, he couldn't do it –but he *was.* Already the decision had been made. He had to meet her again. He had to confirm to himself that the experienced had been real, that he hadn't imagined the whole thing; that it had meant something.

There were some small worn red tiled steps in front of the door, cracked with age, some of the tiles missing, with a small wooden chair cut into the steps. Either side large scaffolding hung, surrounding the door like an ornate black frame. On front of the door was a laminated sign.

AUTOGRPAHS

Members of the company will be happy to sign items from the production –programmes/tickets/books. Please do not ask for anything else to be signed.
One item per person, *either* a signature *or* a photo.
Thank you.

Moses bit his lip and stared at the sign. He knew he was pushing it seeing her again. He was hoping to Christ it would be okay, that the magic would be there again, that he would find that elusive confidence that had come and never been before. He had gotten to the Comedy Theatre for quarter to five, just after the matinée performance. Shortly the people would be making their way around the side of the theatre towards the stage door. He knew the crowd wouldn't be as large as the week before. To accompany the press hammering the audiences had stayed away. The papers had been brutal. The amount of mud the culturally attuned critics of the Sunday and intelligent weeklies had slung at Tessa would have sickened the hearts of her least scrupulous social columnists in Hollywood. In response, Tessa had gone on the instant attack, which had brought out an even more brutal barrage of tabloid responses, the *Guardian* saying – 'Jefford's mortified reaction to the critics reaction lends weight to the idea

127

that she senses the criticism contains more than a grain of truth.' On Tuesday Tessa told the *News of the World* that '… it's a tricky play in many respects because it deals with issues that make people uncomfortable. I don't think that's why the critics aren't liking it. I don't think they're used to this kind of play; they're used to something more traditional that appeals to their sensibility. I've chosen not to read the negative reviews because I don't want it to influence my performance. The response to the play by the audience has been overwhelmingly good. I haven't had a bad experience stage dooring in London. The English are the kindest people I've ever met, literally, so nice. The problem as I see it are the critics. It seems to me that we should do away with the idea of having a press night. It's absolute bollocks as you English like to say, and counter-productive to everyone involved. Somebody has to change the rules, and I guarantee you, the majority of the actors would stand by me –start the petition now!' On Wednesday *The Sun* had a short article in the showbiz section, running pictures of Tessa being very much the girl about town; eating down the Ivy, falling out of the Groucho Club into taxi's, shopping in Regents Street with her new cockney film-editor boyfriend, a young man sporting a heavy beard and retro sepia-tinted spectacles who reminded Moses of the guy in the illustrated guide, *The Joy of Sex.*

Moses continued paced up and down outside the door, muttering under his breath in apprehension, stopping every few seconds to check his watch, each time disappointed that it had hardly changed since the last glance. Around ten past five the people started making their way around the side of the theatre towards the stage door. At half past Tessa appeared. Moses joined the queue as before. He tried to inject confidence into his face, the delirious joy he had felt previous. Instead, he stood nervous, with a shy and timid smile, passing his fingers through his hair, playing with the change in his pocket, waiting impatiently for the other people to finish with their autograph's. He wanted to talk to Tessa, to be a brilliant conversationalist, to surprise her and everybody around with his wit, his penetrating charisma and distinguished ease. He stepped up to her. 'Hi,' he said.

Tessa raised her eyebrows, 'You're returning.'

'Oh, you remember me!' said Moses, a look of genuine surprise on his face, 'you remember *me*? I'm impressed! That you remember me!'

'Yes, I remember you.'

'Oh, you do! That's nice, that you remember me. I mean … that's … that's nice.' He nodded. He looked at her. He nodded. 'Well,' he said, not looking directly at her now, focusing his eyes slightly to the left of her face. 'I'm impressed that you remember me … I mean that's impressive … that you remember me … and … and …it's impressive,' His Adam's apple convulsed. He folded his arms. He unfolded his arms. He tried to smile. The smile came out as a small wrinkle on his lip. He continued sporting the strange wrinkled smile, shifting uncomfortably, hoping that the awkwardness that bathed the moment would be transient.

'I'm impressed that you remember me,' he continued, 'I mean I'm *really* impressed by that … that … you … er.'

He stared at her feebly, politely; and that facile wrinkled smile hung idiotically on his face as he searched the visage of Tessa's features and desperately rummaged the confused closet of his brain for some magic word to ease the tension. 'I wanted to meet you again,' he said, his words chasing and catching each other. 'I wanted to meet you … I mean I want to … I wanted … *wanted*.'

The rest didn't come.

And time went on. And he was standing there in this blank sort of void, his mind going in different directions. He stood there on front of her for several long, long seconds, his mind reeling, his knees trembling. Tessa gazed at him, her expression of cheerfulness broken off and replaced with one of concern. She bit her lip; she made a little laugh. And from that painful confused place, Moses Peartree salvaged a quiet modicum of instinctive dignity. He said: 'I'm so sorry,' and moved on and vanished into the crowd.

He walked around for three or four hours afterwards, longer even, with no hope of knowing what direction he was taking. The traffic was heavy in London. The noise doubled up on itself. The crowds scurried past him on either side of the pavement like a column of ants parting when they encounter an obstacle. He felt broken, shattered really, his heart shrunken inside him and dropping out of his body like a rotten apple. The connection between him and Tessa had vanished. It had started off okay. He remembered that. She had remembered him. That had to mean something, considering all the people she had met between last week and this, all the people she had given autographs to between then and now. He could see she had been expectant, happy to see him again. The recognition in her eyes had shown that. Though he had blown it from the off, not been as relaxed as before, not as funny or as endearing as he had been, and she had noticed. Piecing it together, arguing it out, he should have done the honourable thing and left the second meeting as it was, not gone back to repeat something that was unrepeatable. But he couldn't do that. The sense of not seeing her again had been too much. And now he was paying the price.

It was midnight by the time he got home. He let himself in the door and dragged himself up the stairs with a sad and heavy tread. He paced his bedroom, moaning, muttering in the dark. He reproached himself bitterly for his behaviour. Why had he acted so self-righteously. Why had he been so blasé and said that he was impressed that she remembered him. That is what he had said –*impressed!* He should have allowed a certain decorum, a humility, but instead had gone in there full guns blazing, trying to recreate what had been before. For the rest of the night, he and his brain turned over and over the terrible encounter. He kept on seeing himself standing in front of Tessa at the stage door, his nerves firing, his brain trying to keep control of his feet and knees, looking as nervous as a postman at a dog show. No wonder she had looked at him strangely, that bright smile of hers fading to one of concern. He had wanted so desperately for her to look at him warmly and personably, but no matter how hard he tried he could tell she wasn't impressed. But maybe he was interpreting the whole thing wrongly. Maybe she had been as nervous as he, had longed for his appearance and been unable, like him, to deal with it. Maybe the awkwardness between them was a sign of their attraction for each other. Or maybe she was playing some kind of intricate game with him, some cat and mouse. Maybe she was trying to drive him to return to the theatre, cause a reaction out of him, perform some kind of voodoo influence on him. He felt a great weight lifted from his shoulders at this idea, which lasted for a good twenty minutes before the gloom returned.

131

Finally, exhausted from the day's events, he turned off the light, stumbled his way to the bed, stood over it like a land-mass, went down, and lapsed into a troubled sleep.

Around midday, Moses rose from his bed, bathed, had some breakfast, and took the dog for a walk. He promised himself that he would not see Tessa again, that the whole thing had been a mistake, but that same day, around lunchtime, he grew restless. He had to turn things around. He had to get her to see him the way she had seen him on the second meeting –it was imperative. Shit, he'd even have her see him as he was on the first meeting than have this. He would go and see her one last time and, God willing, resume the whole affair, say that she hoped she remembered him and that she could forgive him and that all he wanted was to apologize to her for being so awkward. He put his books neat and orderly in his room, shaved, dressed, put on his best chequered shirt, and went out the door. He got the early train into London and had a few drinks in Leicester Square. Felt better. Not good. But better – then made his way over to the Comedy Theatre. He arrived there a little after nine, standing to the side of the queue and under the scaffolding. Tessa was already at the stage door, wrapping up for the night and signing the last few autographs. For a moment he thought he saw a weakness in her face. She seemed to be looking anywhere, but in his direction, almost skimming over the space where he stood. He watched her closely, seeing if she would betray any recognition of him, but her eyes studiously avoided his. Then, as if by accident, she looked in his direction. Moses' mind raced at the sudden acknowledgement of his presence. He felt a strange lightning crackle through his veins, and he knew that the gasp in his throat was in her throat, too. She turned away from his look, breaking eye contact as fast as she had made it, and pressed on signing the autographs. Moses left the theatre and went across the road to the pub, ordering a double scotch with ice and sitting at one of the tables. For a long while he sat there without moving, sprawled out upon the table in a kind of dazed stupor. He felt inclined to cry, but he had an instinctive disinclination to letting other people see his tears, and he clenched his teeth to prevent the sobs from escaping. He had been shaken, shaken to the core. He kept seeing Tessa staring at him with that expression of alarm. She had looked nervous, *real* nervous, afraid to even make eye contact with him. The surprise on her face had been unreal. It was akin to panic. What must she have been thinking? Is this guy a nutter? Is this guy going to do something? Have I found my latest stalker? Is that shit running down my legs?

He gulped down the remainder of his drink and stormed out the pub and started wandering around the streets. He wandered distractedly, dully, bumping into things and muttering. At some point he found himself in St. Patrick's Catholic Church. The place was warm and dark, lit by rows of candles that threw a dance of shadows across the floor. He took a place in the front pew and, resting with folded hands, contemplated the altar, watching the long candles burning, the incense curling in blue wreaths upwards towards the ceiling. He arched his neck and stared at the high vaulted ceiling, painted pale blue. He stared at the rows of well-worn pews, the huge pulpit, the massive organ pipes, the imposing representation of the *Pieta.* The smell of incense hung above him, conquering the smell of musk and damp, and a faint blue haze of it clung to the beams, almost hiding the shadowy spaces of the vaulted roof. After an hour, he rose and walked down the nave and out to the street. He made his way back over to the Comedy Theatre, went to the glass doors and pushed them and went inside. He shouted but no one came. He looked at the white statues in the foyer. He couldn't understand why the theatre wasn't locked. He left the theatre and went down the pub across the street, bought a bottle of wine, re-entered the theatre. He passed through the foyer, between statues, and entered the dark auditorium. He sat in an aisle seat and opened the wine. He took out his autographed flyer from his pocket, stood, placed the flyer on the seat, got down on his knees, bowed his head. Then he opened his eyes, raised the bottle of wine, tipped back his head, drank heartily, greedily, and stared at the flyer. When at last he came out the theatre he had finished half of the bottle of wine, emptied the rest of the contents into the street, hailed a taxi and headed back to Waterloo. It was late when he got back home. He didn't turn on the lights but crept to his parents' liquor cabinet, took a bottle of port, and made his way into the kitchen. His mother had left something on the side; bread and sausage, with his favourite American mustard. He ate the bread and sausage with the American mustard, drank the port. Images crowded on him from the night. He sat there with the images, until the bread and sausage was gone and the bottle was empty, then slipped quietly upstairs, pulled off his clothes, put on his paisley pyjamas, got into bed and closed his eyes. He wept disconsolately.

☐

The days and weeks that followed blurred together, and Moses went through them as he might have gone through a driving and nearly unendurable storm, his head down, his jaw locked, his mind fixed upon the next step and the next. Yet for all his stoical endurance and stolid movement through the weeks and days, he was an intensely divided man. One part of him recoiled in instinctive horror at his encounter with Tessa Jefford, and another part drew intensely towards the very tragedy from which he recoiled. It was as if all feeling had been held in abeyance until this certain, fateful moment. And now that moment was here, upon him, and his pain flooded like a drowning wave. He would tread his way through the streets of London, walking up and down, up and down, all the way through the night. He prowled a hundred streets and walked three thousand miles and drank a thousand pints in a thousand pubs. He had never felt such a burning appetite for alcoholic stimulant before. Alone, he had never sought it out; he never bought a bottle for himself; solitary, as his life was, the idea of drinking alone, of whiskey from a flask, filled him with horror. Alcohol, indeed, until his twentieth year had been only a casual and infrequent spirit –once, in his seventeenth year, he had gotten moderately drunk on various liquors which he had mixed together in a tumbler, and drank without discretion. Now, after meeting Tessa he was drinking more than he could ever imagine. It was obvious that the drink, instead of giving him peace or comfort acted as savagely and immediately as oil poured on the tumult of a raging fire –it fed and spurred the madness in him and gave him no release until he had drunk himself into a state of paralyses and stupefaction. He was caught up for the first time in the midst of a great and emotional tide –there was no food that could feed him, no drink that could quench his thirst. Like an insatiate and maddened animal, he roamed the streets of London or prowled through the shelves of high-piled books in his bedroom, tortured by everything he could see and not bring him solace. His obsession for Tessa Jefford had become so intense that it had started overcoming every thought and feeling. His hunger and thirst for her was immense. To make matters worse, the flyer picture could be seen everywhere through London, the same picture of Tessa in a floppy hat and pinned flowers, her face as big as life on the sides of buses, plastered to park stalls, staring from underground escalators. If only she would forgive him for the way he had acted. If only she could understand his sincere and devout love for her. Sometimes it occurred to him he was devoting so much time to a person to whom he had had little social contact, but he quickly drove those thoughts out of his head. He knew people would say it was an infatuation or a crush or transference or some other psychiatric term. He knew that. But it was as if he couldn't help himself. Didn't want to.

One evening in late December, he put on his shoes and oversized corduroy jacket and got the train into London. It was the week before Christmas, and coloured lights flickered on and off in the shop windows. Mock fir trees decked in tinsel stood in pedestrian precincts, and people swarmed in and out of the department stores, looking for happiness in boxes with pretty ribbons and prettier price-tags. He got to the Comedy Theatre around nine and stood in the thick part of the crowd, unnoticed. Tessa was late coming out.

'Where's Tessa then?'

136

'Who knows, probably in some hotel lobby, arguing with the boss over her six-figure bar bill.'
'Yeah, I bet she's holed up in the Hilton pissed as a fart.'

'No, she isn't here yet. Any minute now, they say. You'll tell by the stretch limo. A star? You kidding me? She hasn't been a star since when? Early eighties? Who's interested if she's making a comeback. All right, I'll stop complaining.'

'What a buncha tosh that was! One of the worst theatre experiences I've had!'
'I agree. I found it impossible to stay awake. The man next to me kept nodding off and snoring.'
'Can you blame him?'

Tessa emerged at the stage door at quarter to ten. She looked tired from the days' schedule, her eyes showing a mixture of annoyance and fatigue as she absently brushed at a lock of dirty blonde hair. She waved the people up to her like a herd of sheep, gesturing them to hurry along, sharing secret smiles with her bodyguard as she hastily signed the brochures and programmes. Forgetting the last few people, she headed towards the waiting limo, shoving some of the fans aside like pesky war-torn orphans, slamming the door before the chauffer could even get out the car. The limo shot past Moses on the street as he was adjusting his coat around the waist. In the back of the limousine, barely visible behind tinted glass, a small pale face stared out –the outline of cheekbones, a high milky brow, a slight almost vestigial mouth, the nape of a white neck visible under a half halo of blonde hair. The limo sped away, picking up speed as it cruised into traffic of the West

End. Moses wiped his mouth, wrung his hands, buttoned his corduroy jacket up to the neck, and followed the disappearing taillights of the limo, two red eyes in the darkness.

As the days and weeks passed, Moses' thoughts dwelt less and less on Tessa Jefford. He started to come to terms with the fact he had imagined the smile she had given him to be something far exceeding an ordinary connection. How stupid of him to have thought that she had liked him in that way; how stupid to have imagined she had 'those kinds' of feelings towards him. He looked back on the last few weeks with slight bemusement. He could not understand how he had submitted to the dishonor of such an infatuation, and in a sense, he was angry at Tessa for the way she had made him feel. He had been infatuated with a person that had never once uttered a syllable of his name, nor did a single atom of her mind or perfectly sculptured body care for his existence on this forsaken earth. He had let a fleeting reaction influence his entire life. In addition, the whole theatre world didn't look the same to him anymore. Whereas before, the theatre-goers looked assured and self-possessed, now they looked egotistical, glib, and dishonest, without talent and without sincerity, with nothing, in fact, except a feeble incapacity for the shock and agony of life, and a desire to escape into a glamorous and unreal world of make believe; a justification for their pitiable and base existence –it's a wonder anybody could stand being around them, such people.

One Saturday in mid-January, he decided to take the dog for a walk over the fields the other side of his old secondary school. As he passed the newspaper vending machine at the shop, he caught a glimpse of the morning headlines.

HAS-BEEN ACTRESS
GOES ALL OUT
AFTER BACKSTAGE ALTERCATION

Placing a coin in the vending machine, he took out a paper and stared at the picture under the headline. Tessa Jefford was being escorted by two theatre staff out of the Comedy Theatre and into an ambulance. It read:

A fight broke out last night backstage of the Comedy Theatre in one of the most extraordinary occurrences of what one might call a 'thespian debacle.' The street at the side of the theatre was choked with scenes of strangeness as the *Private Investigators in Space* star Tessa Jefford was dragged out the stage door and placed into a waiting ambulance. There are no reports of what actually took place, only that words escalated to fists between Jefford and her soon-to-be-husband-number-seven –Dexter Rhys-Brooks –whilst Jefford was receiving cards and flowers from the theatre crew in her dressing room. After the barrage of discouraging reviews, the curtain had fallen on the penultimate performance of Richard Richards disappointingly received *Last Tango in Paris,* running for only eight weeks out of its prescribed twelve to poor houses. Cast, crew, and significant others were saying their goodbyes and letting loose together one final time in the grand tradition of the 'cast party'. After a few moments of waxing nostalgically over the eight-week run, the apparent tussle took place between Jefford and her fiancé. Rumor has it Jefford had been drinking champagne with her co-star Alan Rogers all day long, going down the pub next to the theatre – the Tom Cribb –between matinée and evening performances, to, as thespians put it –'wet the whistle.' When she and Rogers returned to the theatre, everyone could see they were markedly inebriated, and Jefford had supposedly taken a dislike to something one of the female members of the company said. Jefford had hurled abuse at the girl, at which, her soon-to-be-husband had retaliated by defending the female crew member. It was then that the supposed altercation took place between Jefford and her fiancé. Harsh words were exchanged and bystanders were caught in a hail of champagne bottles as Jefford and her fiancé fought it out, with several people being injured in the fight, one of them being Jefford's agent. Several sources describe Jefford going into some kind of breakdown. Her agent summoned the best private physician in London – a Dr. Herbert Wolfgang Heiz – who hurried to the dressing room, arriving only seconds after Jefford, with strong assistance from valium, had stumbled onto the stage and collapsed while the theatre hands were cleaning up for the night. Two theatre workers, looking very much under duress, were seen escorting the shaken Jefford out the stage door and into an ambulance. A few reporters who were waiting to take some pictures of Jefford's final autograph session, caught the whole fracas in a series of sensational photos, which show Jefford behaving like a maniac as she is dragged from the theatre whilst the crowds look on in curious bemusement. According to another source, the semi-conscious Jefford has been taken to a private hospital in Harley Street, where she has been kept under heavy sedation for the next forty-eight hours. The Comedy Theatre has postponed her final performance.

As Moses read the article his spirit began to emerge from the blanket of shame and sick despair that had covered it over the last few weeks. He felt dislocated – so many constructs exploding in so few minutes. He began to laugh, a long careful laugh, he realized he hadn't laughed in years. He woke early the next morning with a clear decision. *He was going to write his book.* After all these years he was finally getting around to writing his long-awaited *opus*. He got up before light, and sitting at the bureau, with pen and writing pad, started scribbling furiously. For three whole hours the pen moved across the paper as if had a life of its own. Then he took a break, had a shower, and waited for the dawn.

Don't Drop the Salad Cream

The great army of apes. God's chosen ones. All hanging upside down. A mass crucifixion of monkeys, a veritable slaughter of simians, barely visible behind extremely shitty fire effects. It's early. It's *real* early. Three forty-seven in the morning to be exact. Waking up this early should be illegal. Waking up in general is a difficult task in itself, it's like the second hardest thing in the world, if you know what I mean. So here I am awake at three forty-seven in the morning, yawning, scratching, hands clutching around genitals under pyjama bottoms as I watch gorillas being crucified on inverted crosses surrounded by shitty sheets of flame and black smoke. I don't sleep that much on a Friday night if I'm honest with you anyway, knowing I have to get up early for work the next day. Maybe two, three hours, the most. I'll tell you something weird, I can't even masturbate, it's something to do with prospect of all that seriousness that's lying ahead of me; the chicken won't let itself get chocked because of all that shit I'm going to have to deal with later. Anyway, let me tell you why I'm awake at this ungodly hour. They're currently showing all five *Planet of the Apes* films on Saturday mornings between three and five a.m. The one they're showing this morning is *Beneath the Planet of the Apes*, the second one of the films, the one where the subterranean genetically altered beings with telepathic powers blow up the world at the end. The first film is obviously the best, the one with Charlton Heston in it. The second one, the one that's on tonight – also with Charlton Heston in it, though his part is much smaller, to a degree–has the basic premise as the first film: astronauts crash on planet, captured by apes, costume change from retro-cool spacesuit to caveman loincloth; revelation that the ape planet was earth all along. You can practically skip the fifty-minute mark of *Beneath* without missing anything important, but there are a few moments that stick with you, like the choir-singing genetically altered beings singing in the underground ruins of New York, or the ships' captain of the crashed spaceship giving a death rattle that starts the film off with an all-encompassing depressive yet somehow touching whimper. Apart from that the film is sort of bollocks. Plus, everybody dies at the end; the apes, Charlton Heston, the genetically altered beings with telepathic powers – everyone's toast. Apparently, Charlton Heston insisted to the producers that his character dies at the end of the film. I mean can you imagine an actor insisting his character dies in a sequel? Hey, hello! Think of the money, bud! Although Leonard Nimoy did die at the end of *Star Trek II.* But

144

when I think of it, neither of them actually *died* died. They lived on in the sequels.

My intention is to record all five ape films on VHS tape. I've bought two 240 minutes cassettes for the first four films, and a 120 minutes cassette for the last film. The recording went quite well last week, although I recorded it on a Scotch tape, the lower end of the spectrum of blank tapes. It's a bit fuzzy the quality –a bit like the apes' hair –but the sound's not bad, as is the color. I usually stick to the higher-grade tapes like TDK or BASF. The next level down from that is Sony, then Maxell, then Sharp, then Scotch, and finally TDK's low-level series. Anything after that are not worth the mention, they're worse than Kodak, although Kodak is off the spectrum of crappiness. The reason I'm staying up to record the films and not placing them on timer is because I want to cut out the adverts. I can't stand a good flick being intruded upon by the Milk Tray man jumping out a window or somebody's mother whipping up Angel Delight in the kitchen. I've developed a finely-honed instinct when it comes to adverts and when they are about to start, like sometimes I need to go for a slash, but my instincts are telling me a break is on its way, so I just have to hold it in and wait. I must admit, I've got the whole thing down to a tee now. When I first started cutting out adverts there would be a few seconds of wobbling sounds, and the picture would go snowy, but now there's a nice clean cut, well –nearly clean. Occasionally, I get the face of the Rice Krispies monkey or the red curly head of Ronald McDonald, but more or less I'm quite good at editing now. Most of the films in my collection are films that have been recorded from TV. The qualities not bad in actual fact. Sometimes you can't see the difference between the recording and the broadcast. Occasionally, you get the halo effect over heads, but nothing that can't be solved with a little twiddling of the tracking knob, and it beats the pirate copies where the quality is laughable. All in all, everything has come out quite well, except for *El Cid* which has a long white crackling line that works its way steadily up the screen from start to finish, periodically obscuring Charlton Heston's face. Nonetheless, I must say, Sophia Loren's tits look quite good broken in half. I have about three hundred cassettes in my personal collection now, and about that many doubles and other cassettes, which I picked up at thrift shops, garage sales, and flea markets. I have action, animation, crime, drama, comedy, horror, satire, western, urban, documentaries, epics, science fiction, fantasy, magical realism, mum's Corrie. If possible, I like to print off the labels for the cassette jackets, preferably New Times Roman. In the early days the whole thing was a confused mess of carboard cases and labels scribbled over countless times with biro, there was nowhere else to scribble, but the cardboard sleeves. Sometimes I had DON'T TAPE OVER in big bold capitals on the label, and there was nothing on the cassette. Even the dog had its own cassette. In the end I stripped all the cassettes of their labels and used a little square numbering system and worked the whole lot into an index. I suppose you could say the whole thing is a bit obsessive. My parents say they don't like me watching too much TV, thinks it confuses me when I should be playing some sort of sport or going out with friends. They always seem to be having a go at me over something or other, telling me I'm wearing the wrong colour socks or I don't know how to smile for the camera. They recently said I needed to start pulling my weight around the house, like my sister did getting that job in the Italian restaurant down by the lights. My sister's been delegated the responsible one out of the two of us. I suppose they've got a point about me. I may be a little superficial in a sense, a little on the lazy side, content to stay in and watch the box whilst pick my feet and fart under the covers. My dad keeps saying he can't get much volume out of me, whatever that means, says watching TV is a wastage of time activity, tells me I should take up rugby or scouts or some other outdoorsy activity. It's because of this lack of social energy that my parents advised me I get a Saturday job. That's why I'm working as a supermarket assistant in Sainsbury's over the Christmas. I suppose the job isn't too bad in the circumstances. And I don't want you to think I've done anything wrong there, at least anything *seriously* wrong, unless you call pissing in the disabled toilets seriously wrong. It's just that I'm not feeling the place, not digging the karma of it, for want of a better phrase. Plus, there's this little thing that happened to me last week. In fact, I don't know if I should even call it a little thing, more like a big deal.

Before I get to it, I'll tell you how I got the job. It was a sunny afternoon about a month ago and I was in my bedroom swapping the tape spool of the shop rental copy of *Raiders of the Lost Ark* over with the tape spool of my own second-hand copy –quite a feat, even if I say so myself –when my dad came in and proceeded to thrust against my nose what proved to be an advert from the local newspaper, which was at once withdrawn so that I might read it. It said there was Saturday work going at the Sainsburys store in the high street, a nice glossy two-page spread asking for part-time staff above a bottle of Sainsburys red and a slice of cheddar. So, I applied for the job, was *made* to by my parents, not really expecting anything from it, but a couple of days later, literally a couple of days later I got a phone call from Sainsbury's about coming in for an interview and I was like, okay, yeah, sure, if you like. The interview was nine in the morning on a Wednesday. It was like two days later, so I was really glad it wasn't a week later because then I would've been a bit worried about it. Also, I kind of knew someone who had worked at Sainsbury's for a couple of months so I asked them whether it was a good place to work and they asked who my interview was with and I said it was a Mr. Hardly and they said he was the nicest manager I could ever hope for and I must admit, he, Mr. Hardly, seemed really nice on the phone so that helped me a lot and I'm glad it wasn't a woman because women intimidate me. So I went along to the interview and the receptionist said, she told me, oh, there's been a lot of you in today and I was, like, awesome, so there's been a lot of us in today so I probably won't get the job, and then I saw Mr. Hardly and as soon as he said hello I was, like, a lot more relaxed because he was okay and we went into this big room and for some reason this made it a lot more scary and I thought it was the weirdest thing he didn't ask me many questions but basically called me in to give me the job. I was offered a temp position for eight weeks, commencing on Saturday till the first week in January. Mr. Hardly told me that it would be super busy over the Christmas and that there was the option of getting trained on checkouts as they always needed people on checkouts and that I'll get a lot of hours on the run up to Christmas, time, and time and a half. I was given an employment handbook and locker, issued a pair of brown slim-fit trousers, a white shirt, two white short-sleeved shirts, a clip-on tie, also brown, and a pair of spongey-souled black shoes that looked like they were cast-offs from C&A. Apart from that, everything seemed to be tickety-boo. I wasn't sure about my work colleagues though. I don't think I'm very good with people. That was one of the things that had worried me about the job, you know, how I would deal with the co-workers and, if I worked with the public, how I would deal with that. Personally, I'd rather have a job where I'm not dealing with people, like, I don't have to deal with people, like, I'm not *having* to deal with people. I can't stand the old ladies and shit, especially the ones that come in on the Saturday's. They always seem to be having a grumpy over something or other and seem to regard you as a zookeeper might regard an obnoxious specimen, like they want to piss on you from a lofty height. I had to explain the other week to some old biddy that the Cornish pasties had got lost in transit and she kept on having a go like it was my fault, getting all upset and telling me could I please hurry up and help her before her parking meter ran out. Anyway, back to the reason I'm leaving the job. It happened last week. I was on the shop floor, cleaning up and getting everything ready, being busy or trying to look busy which to me is the same thing, and this woman, this woman from up north, one of the senior management who's always pushing me to be more customer focused, told me to go and start replenishing the shelves, so I went and done that, what she said. I'd just got this box of salad cream jars to put on a top shelf, and here it is, I decided to save some time and lift the whole lot in one go, to impress everyone, especially the woman from up north, so I started lifting this heavy box of salad cream's when –wham –I lost my grip … dropped them … poured the whole lot over the free-range turkeys. A bloody mess it was, it turned out to be. The salad cream jars shattered to bits … literally shards of glass everywhere. Just lovely, Christmas turkeys mingled

149

with everybody's favorite salad dressing. So, anyway, I started cleaning it up, scrapping the excess salad cream off the turkeys when I looked around and saw that woman from up north. She was watching me real close, looking down at her clipboard and then looking back at me and I was kind of getting nervous. And I sort of spilt some of the salad cream down my shirt and my voice went … churrrrrhh –and I went … *shit*! And suddenly I remembered that I wasn't supposed to swear, and I said *fuck*! And it was like something out of a film, it was so stupid, and everything went wrong … for that reason. Everybody was really pathetic about it afterwards, having a decent laugh I mean. I had to explain the story like eighteen thousand times because – oopsie, I dropped the salad cream. I guess they'll never make a musical out of it. So, there you are. There you have it. There you go. That's why I'm giving up the job. The whole salad cream business pissed me right off.

You know what I'd like to do? You know what I'd like to do when I leave the job? I'd like to pick up a rock and throw it at the place. Stupid, right? Like a damn kid. I'd like to pick up a rock and wing it against the building, symbolic of my disapproval of supermarket chains and the food retail sector, so to speak. I guess that if I could knock off one-sixteenth of a square inch of the place, destroy just that much of it, it would be enough for the time being. But I doubt I'll have the balls to do it. Maybe I'll just run a bogie along the window some time. Anyway, I think I might call it a night, get some sleep before I go in, a few hours at least, let the tape run to the end.

Aww – ain't that sweet, a mother gorilla is holding a baby ape in her arms, just like that statue by

Michelangelo. Is it me or does Cornelius look like
Maradona?

A
Card
From Haifa

We have huts –or chalets. It is a simple space, with
cardboard walls and doors of paper screens.
The central part of the hut, which is the only place in
which a tall man can stand erect, is not over seven feet
wide; there is a single window at the front of where
stands a table. I have a couple of straight chairs, a
narrow bed pushed in under some low shelving. It could
literally be said that I crawl into bed. In the left corner
is the little heap of my possessions –a cagoule, a
knapsack, a torch, some socks, a novel on Scandinavian
art in the dark ages. The rest of the room is reserved for
bacteria. At night the air is solid with wood. Sometimes
I get a camp chair and place it outside the hut and read

there by a single unshaded bulb, or turn it out and sit listening to the distant traffic, and the human antihuman noises that come up from the batch of track houses across the way and woodlands further on, and wheat fields still further, beyond the underdeveloped spaces of the land and the western reach of the fence. On these nights, I listen in an uninvolved way to the far traffic east of me, to the flurry of night bird, to an occasional owl between me and the main house. And I remember the fullness of the sun during the day, the hot potted flowers on the doorsteps, the washing hanging from balconies, girls in doorways sitting on chairs with their hair in curlers reading magazines, the road, hard and white, searing the tender pastures, climbing through miles of well-kept avocado and grapefruit orchards and endless lemon groves, all to be watered and cared for. To the north the high, vast hills are covered with trees and bushes, purple and yellow flowers, to the east there are no trees; it is barren there, every rock as it must have been for a thousand years, an immense space of immeasurable silence. There is much work available here, including factory, gardening, children's house, kitchen, avocado groves. Most of the work is rotated on a temporary basis, although volunteers do most of the worst jobs, at least until they have proved that they are well behaved and/or show skills for some other more interesting work. Food is abundant and of a reasonable quality. I receive three meals a day taken in the communal dining room. The emphasis is on vegetables, fruit and dairy products. Breakfasts consists of self-service salads, cheese, eggs, yoghurts, bread, tea, coffee, milk and chocolate. Lunch is hot and consists of soup, meat or meat substitute, fish, pasta, vegetables, salad and fruit juice. The evening meal is similar to the breakfast with self-service salads and the occasional hot

152

dish. I drink alcohol whenever I can, in the volunteers hut, in front of the volunteers hut, down at the beach, supping vodka and Goldstar and watching the sun go down over the rustic cabins that dot the grassy hills, the red and white curtains blowing in and out of the one-storied houses in the most abandoned fashion. They celebrated Purim here last week, a new experience for me. The classrooms of the schools turned into bedouin tents, everybody going with their costumes to the dining hall. There were electric guitars and pink girls in miniskirts. Men blasted on trumpets, accordions, washtubs, spoons, beer glasses, rattles. Pots of flowers hung from the ceiling; there was sawdust on the floor, the walls were covered in murals of fruit and farming scenes. The locals sang melodiously, playing on tuneful instruments, or indulging in those pleasant games played with cards, dice, or cups. There was a lot of spilling over into the gardens afterwards to watch something on TV –dim and grainy –an old film. I left as they were clearing the tables and went out on the balcony and sniffed the pines below, listened to the flying insects, watched a lark fluttering overhead, leaned over and looked to the north. A black cloud had blown in off the hills there, but a faint glow of yellow and gold still trailed in the east. I gazed at the hills, then at the gardens, then at the road, and back to the hills, and then lifted my eyes into the very centre of the sky. The ribbon of yellow gold had no apparent source up there. I could only think that from somewhere above, unseen, perhaps to the left, light streamed through where the clouds was thin, unless of course, this yellow light was being sucked up –to me, seemed to be imploring or seeking guidance. Too wise now to interrupt or question, I let my gaze above, and did not move. At first, in that bit of blackness, I could make out

153

a single star, but now I saw them plainly, and there was three parallel, and there was what *must* be a –planet. I have no clear recollection of the day following this other than the weather was bright and warm and I was all the time feeling like I had sinkers attached to my body and all over, huge metal weights. On the Saturday, I took the bus into Haifa and bought a postcard of the beach, which I sent to my parents.

The Resurrection of Urbain Grandier

A Play in one Act

THE RESURRECTION OF URBAIN GRANDIER

(*Characters*)

URBAIN GRANDIER, *the ghost.*
TOM HASTIE, *the traveler.*

The action of the Play passes in the town of Loudun in the year 1934.

SCENE — *The main setting, which stands throughout the play has a cyclorama backing. Provided in the flies are suitable flats or cut-outs, which are lowered as required, representing a public square, a hotel room, and a walled garden. At the opening of the play the stage represents the public square. Surrounding the square are small stone houses scattered around a church.*

Before the CURTAIN *rises, the musical piece – Parson's Farewell, on mandolin – is heard. This continues softly for some time after the play has commenced.*

When the CURTAIN *rises, the stage is in darkness. The* LIGHTS *come up on the setting. It is late afternoon in the small provincial town of Loudun in France. A streetlamp shines weakly in the public square, casting a pane of yellow light across the church doors. The musical piece continues. A young man in high boots, breeches, headscarf, carrying a rucksack and walking stick, enters from the right of stage. This is* TOM HASTIE. *He stands for a moment in the square, looking around. The music ceases. The chimes of the church tower strike quarter to seven, and before they have finished, one can hear footsteps. From the left of stage, a man advances, carrying a branch of laurel in his hands. He is wearing a claret-colored doublet and starched ruff, reminiscent of the early seventeenth century. Thick black wavy hair hangs from a belted felt hat –like a Quakers hat, and an elegant Van Dyke beard adorns his chin. The doublet and ruff are slightly worn and frayed at the edges. This is* **URBAN GRANDIER.** *He looks* TOM *over, stroking his Van Dyke beard in an exaggerated manner.*

158

GRANDIER

Hmm. Interesting. Yes, very amusing. I've never met anyone quite like you before. I see you are a stranger to these parts.

TOM

I am a traveler, sir. Making my way down to Poitiers. And who might you be?

(*A ludicrous expression of astonishment spreads over Grandier's face*)

GRANDIER

Why, I am Father Urbain Grandier, parson and confessor of this church you stand before–or was.

TOM

Was?

GRANDIER

Yes, you see I am not of this world.

TOM

You are not of *this* world?

GRANDIER

Yes, I am deceased.

TOM

Deceased! You mean you are dead?

GRANDIER

I mean dead. Precisely.

(Tom gives a small, uncertain laugh.)

GRANDIER
You don't believe me?

TOM
Please pardon me. I have never met a dead person
before.

GRANDIER
It is perfectly true. Can you not see? My pallor shows I
have less blood than any man.

(Tom looks at Grandier's face more closely.)

TOM
You look very much alive to me.

GRANDIER
Shame on you for making fun of me, sir. You are a
miserable wretch! I tell you I am dead!

TOM
But if you don't believe me, I will be happy to bring
you a mirror.

GRANDIER
I want no mirror. Nor do I think any could be brighter
than the one in which I am looking at myself now –my
conscience!

*(Grandier advances towards Tom, grasping his hand
tightly, as though afraid he might leave)*

GRANDIER

Tell me. Do you believe a man is permitted to admit to a crime he has not committed, even under the duress of torture?

TOM

No.

GRANDIER

That is what the people of this town attempted have me do.

TOM

What do you mean?

GRANDIER

It was here in this church, in the year of Our Lord sixteen hundred and thirty-four, that I was condemned to die a most cruel death for being a practitioner of the black arts. I was accused of being responsible for the possession of certain sisters of the Holy Order of St. Ursula. With one voice these spouses of Christ accused me of having thrown a spell on them and being the cause of their ruin. The authorities accepted without question the false testimony of these women, believing that the Devil under constraint of exorcism, was bound to tell truth. I maintained that I was innocent throughout the hearing and that I was wrongly accused of the charges. I refused to acknowledge myself guilty of sorcery under torture, stating always that I was no magician and that the only magic I had practiced was that of the act of Communion. Despite maintaining my innocence throughout, I was condemned as a companion of hell, and my unkind countrymen placed

161

me at the stake to perish, burned in front of the largest crowd this town had seen for the crime of consorting with the Devil.

(Tom drops his eyes, trying to disguise his skepticism.)

TOM

Well, now. That's interesting … fascinating even … unusual definite.

GRANDIER

You are not convinced of my story?

TOM

Being burned at the stake is one thing, but returning from the ashes is another.

GRANDIER

I understand your surprise of this my son. No doubt you are completely unaware that such an occurrence is possible.

TOM

But the dead do not rise —or at least not yet. Come now. You know I am a stranger to these parts. Be honest and honorable with me, sir. Who are you?

GRANDIER

My name is Urbain Grandier and I am dead.

TOM

As you said. But this is mere foolishness. How could such a thing be true. And if such a thing were true, how might I know it.

GRANDIER

Do you doubt your senses?

TOM

Perhaps. I am aware that I am in a town of deep antiquity. For all I know you are a manifestation brought on by the religious significance of the place, similar to the miracles of St. Bernardino of Siena, or the Marian apparitions witnessed by various shepherd girls in France. Perhaps you are a miracle or perhaps a fantasy caused by an unconscious spiritual yearning in me, a hallucination precipitated by the cultural fabric of the landscape. I surmise the latter.

GRANDIER

But I *tell* you I am dead! For the love of God, be patient and give ear to what I have to say. I was myself once as you; and felt pity for those who believed such stories. Whereas I now find that I myself am to be pitied as much, at least, as experience has instructed me otherwise.

(Grandier pauses, raises his hand and touches his cheek, casts his eyes about the square, leans in towards Tom.)

GRANDIER

Pray, sir, are you of the Catholic faith?

TOM

I am a Calvinist.

GRANDIER

Ah, a Huguenot! That is a pity. Still, this may yet be of use to me, though I disagree with much of their doctrine, there is nevertheless some that makes sense. You see there is something I must ask you to do for me.

TOM

What is it you require?

GRANDIER

If it pleases God, I ask that you make an offering in silver, along with three pounds of wax and the tolling of the church bells for my soul in this church over the next three days and nights.

TOM

Why so?

GRANDIER

I have been caught in Purgatory these last three centuries and need your prayers to depart from there. The year is nineteen hundred and thirty-four, I understand?

TOM

Yes.

GRANDIER

And the date is August the sixteenth?

TOM

It is.

GRANDIER

Then this Saturday will exactly be precisely three-hundred years since my execution. I am allowed every hundred years to wander this earth for the three nights leading up to my burning. Unfortunately, the two times I have visited here before I was met by children who were beaten by their parents for telling idle tales. It is imperative I meet someone this time who I can trust, for whoever I meet this time will seal my fate forever. On this Saturday, if prayers are not said for my soul, the gates of heaven will be closed to me, and I will be condemned to live an eternity in Purgatory. (*Grandier's voice trembles*) I beseech thee, I implore thee, sir, in the spirit of Christian brotherhood, that you undertake these prayers for me!

(Slight pause.)

TOM

If you wish.

GRANDIER

That is good. The exercise must be done at midnight and again in early morning. Two repetitions of it should be made at the times of mass and vespers, finishing with three colloquies to Our Lady, the Son, and the Father.

(Tom scratches his head. Grandier looks at him with an apologetic smile.)

165

GRANDIER

You must think I am terribly fussy. But it is imperative
that you remember to do these things in their order.

TOM

I will attend to the details.

GRANDIER

I pray that love, victorious in heaven and on earth, will
place upon your soul the importance of this
undertaking. I will appear in this square every evening
for the next three nights at the stroke of the last quarter
before the hour of seven. Please say you will meet me
here.

(Tom nods.)

GRANDIER

Very well, I bid you good night.

*(Grandier bows, tilt's his hat, puts his cloak about him
and takes his leave, making his way to the left of the
stage. Before disappearing, he turns and says –)*

GRANDIER

And see that the candles be not forgotten, nor the
tolling of the church bell.

TOM

I pledge you my solemn word.

*(Grandier disappears. The lights on the stage dim to
BLACK-OUT. Tom stands quietly for a minute in the
darkness. The three walls of a room are dropped in*

166

from the flies. The LIGHTS *come up on a hotel room. The room is spacious, dimly lit, quietly, elegantly furnished. There are two Jacobean chairs by the bed. A Bible, and several prayer books are on a table near a crystal decanter of wine. On one wall hangs an oil-painting of the Madonna and Child, faded and almost defaced with age.* GRANDIER *and* TOM *enter from the right.)*

TOM

Please, have a chair. But first, let me take your hat.

GRANDIER

You are most kind. I should not have worn a cloak. It is warm this evening.

(Tom takes Grandier's hat and cloak and Grandier moves to one of the chairs and sits, unbuttoning his doublet. Tom crosses to the decanter of wine, fills two glasses, and hands one to Grandier.)

GRANDIER

This town is considerably smaller than I remember it. I never thought I would see it in such a diminutive state.

TOM

It's certainly quiet here.

GRANDIER

I remember it when it was a magnificent city, with turrets … defensive towers … draw-bridges … the walls were a remarkable white stone. Physically, I would say it has lost some of its former beauty.

167

TOM

Nothing abides forever.

GRANDIER

Quite so.

(Grandier smiles and takes a sip of wine.)

GRANDIER

I couldn't help being taken by these aut-o-mo-biles of yours. They strike me as being one of the most astonishing achievements of your age. But pray tell, what is there usage?

TOM

For travel, of course.

GRANDIER

In what sense?

TOM

To make one's journey faster.

(Grandier looks puzzled.)

GRANDIER

By God's wounds, why would you want that?

TOM

To save time.

(Grandier waves both arms towards heaven.)

GRANDIER

May all the saints have mercy upon us. The world has become a clock!

(*Grandier laughs, genuinely amused by his own cynicism. There is a pause as they sup their wines.*)

GRANDIER

That was a lovely thing you did for me this evening. I am deeply grateful.

TOM

You are welcome.

GRANDIER

You were very generous as to invite me to dine with you. It is the first invitation I have received in the last three hundred years, and I, who have sat down with meat with the most distinguished scholars of my age. I must confess that I miss a little social intercourse.

TOM

I hope the food was to your liking.

GRANDIER

Very much, especially the soup *à la marseillaise*, although in my day there was a great deal more onion in it.

TOM

I heard it was a highly cherished dish of the court of Louis XIII.

GRANDIER

Indeed, it was. There used to be a good dining house in this town when I was alive, just behind the church, an ancient inn with Gallic windows and breasty waitresses. They used to sing when they greeted me. Everything was always ready in the kitchen. The mayors' plump wife was a choosy trollop.

(*Grandier leans back in his chair, takes a huge swallow of wine and smacks his lips.*)

GRANDIER

You know. I have never met a foreigner who spoke such perfect French as you.

TOM

Thank you. I had a good tutor at Eton.

GRANDIER

I have heard such good things about that school. Were you happy there?

TOM

Not much. I felt like an average-sized fish in a much larger pond.

(*Grandier smiles ironically.*)

GRANDIER

I understand your sentiments. My childhood was much the same. You are of English blood?

TOM

Scottish.

GRANDIER

Is the food as bad as they say there?

TOM

Beastly.

GRANDIER

Don't you find that part of the world cold?

TOM

Sometimes. As a matter of fact, I only spend half the year there, I prefer Italy.

GRANDIER

Ah!– glorious country! I applaud your discernment, although I fear their wine is of an inferior quality to ours. The French wine is the finest in the world. It is in the taste you see … it is all in the taste. Italian wines don't taste much different from one another. I don't know whether it is the soil or the climate or something else. But I suspect it is the fault of the Italians themselves. The Italian worker does not give a hoot about what he is working at. He has no interest in his work. Now the French worker will often beg his employer may he stay overtime to make the wine perfect. Because what he is doing, he loves. The French want to make the wine perfect. The Italians, they don't care, they don't caress the grapes, they don't care for the grapes, they don't *love* the grapes.

TOM

They may have inferior wine, but they did produce Da Vinci.

GRANDIER

Oh, *him*. Yes, for sure, he was one of their better exports. A great painter –dreadfully underrated.

(They sit for a moment in silence, sipping their wine, ruminating.)

TOM

So, Reverend sir, tell me of Purgatory. I must confess I had doubts such a place existed. The notion of an intermediate realm between heaven and hell, and the system of indulgences meant to relieve the sufferings of the souls imprisoned within, seem quite absurd to me; a mere remnant of an ancient tradition, or perhaps a convenient means of the Church to obtain money from its flock.

GRANDIER

Spoken like a true Calvinist.

TOM

But I still do not understand your reasons for being there. What crimes have you committed for being sent to such a place? What were your sins for being consigned to such a Dantean underworld? It wasn't your fault the injustices that were committed against you. If anything, you should have been sanctified.

(Grandier puts down his glass, a disturbed look on his face.)

GRANDIER

It is late. I must take my leave of you.

TOM

No. Why don't you have a nightcap? I insist. I have a very fine wine from the Bergerac region.

(Grandier rises from his chair and crosses to the window, his hands behind his back. He stands for a minute before the window. Tom stares at him and tilts his head, puzzled by his sudden change of mood.)

TOM

Is something wrong?

(Grandier turns from the window and speaks solemnly.)

GRANDIER

I remember while a student at Bordeaux, a monk was burned for sorcery, but the clergy and the fellow monks did their best to save him, even though he had made a confession of his crime. *(He pauses, closes his eyes.)* I can see him now, that monk, shouting against our Savior and the world. I see his distorted face through the roaring curtain of flames – *'Jesu! Jesu! Jesu!'* And then the screams becoming inarticulate … becoming the screams of a frightened animal … and there was nobody to take mercy … nobody to put an end to the agony.

(Grandier's face takes on an expression of anguish.)

TOM

I am sorry for what you have gone through, Father, and still go through.

GRANDIER

Death meets us everywhere my child, and is procured
by every instrument and in all chances, and enters in at
many doors –by violence!

*(There is a pause. Grandier composes himself, a new
resolve in his voice.)*

GRANDIER

I must speak frank with you, good sir. Before I depart
tonight, there is something you must learn about me. I
have ventured to form an opinion of you. It is highly
favorable. I believe you are an honest and honorable
gentleman. I trust you know me well enough for you to
permit me this frankness.

TOM

Go ahead. *(slightly nervous.)*

*(Grandier comes forward and reaches out his hand.
Tom hesitates, then takes the hand. The dead priest
fixes him with large, dark eyes.)*

GRANDIER

Do you remember how on that night on the Mount of
Olives, Our Lord lifted his arms to heaven and cried –
Father, let this cup be taken from me?

TOM

Yes, of course.

GRANDIER

He was afraid you see, *very* afraid. But he seized the cup and drank it down in one swallow.

(Releasing Tom's hand, Grandier starts pacing the room, resolutely.)

GRANDIER

I have to tell you something, something I haven't told you since our meeting yesterday. I had my own moment of weakness on the Mount of Olives.

(Grandier stops pacing, pours himself another wine, swirls the wine in the glass, stares into its depths.)

GRANDIER

I have told you of the authorities attempts at using the Ursuline nuns as a means by which to destroy me.

TOM

You have.

GRANDIER

I had made an enemy of certain people in France, certain powerful people, notably that of Cardinal Richelieu.

(Grandier takes a half-hearted mouthful of wine. He looks nervous.)

GRANDIER

The King under Richelieu had resolved to raze the castles and fortresses existing in the heart of the Kingdom as a means of ensuring peace in France after the religious wars. This required that all the strongholds be demolished. They commissioned a special envoy, a

Jean de Laubardemont to see to the demolition of that of Loudun. I opposed the act publicly, criticizing and satirizing the Cardinal and his actions. I did everything I could to frustrate his destructive plans. As a consequence, I was arrested on the constructed charge of possessing and debauching the Holy Order of St. Ursula.

TOM

And the nuns' accusations, they were false?

GRANDIER

Mere fabrication! The whole affair was a hoax orchestrated by Richelieu. To think that people actually believed that in this town devils had gathered to wage war on God by the use of magic –such childishness!

(Grandier makes a contemptuous laugh. He stares into the shadows, grips his wine glass.)

GRANDIER

I was arrested and confined to the prison at Angers. For four months I languished there. During that time, I was a model of patience and firmness, passing my days in reading good books or in writing prayers and meditations. Later, I was moved to a top floor of the house of a Father Mignon in Loudun, which was small with blocked windows. There under lock and key, I was allowed to see no one, allowed to read nothing, without even a candle to light the darkness. I remained there for some weeks. The heat was horribly oppressive. The terror of what was to befall me became unbearable. I cried aloud in the cell, lying there in the hot darkness, crying in the night, like a woman, like a frightened child. I clenched my fists, I gritted my teeth, I vowed to

176

myself that nobody should ever call me a coward. Let them do their worst! I was ready for it! Alas, the flesh is strong, but the spirit is weak!

(Grandier takes a fierce gulp of wine.)

GRANDIER

At the reading of my sentence, I maintained that I had never been a sorcerer or known any other magic except that of holy scripture. I acknowledged my Savior and prayed that the blood of his passion may save me. Then I pleaded with the judges to moderate the severity of my punishment, in fear that during the torments that awaited me I would not be overcome with despair and cease to have hope in the mercy of God. I asked the judges that they would be so pleased to mitigate, if only a little of the rigor of punishment, for the sake of my soul unless it lapsed in its faith. To avoid my souls' eternal damnation, Jean de Laubardemont decided that I was to be strangled before my body was caught up in the flames, dependent on me obtaining his favor by confessing that I was guilty of the crime of magic. I responded I had never committed such a crime and thus was taken away to torture and death.

(Grandier's chest swells with anger.)

GRANDIER

I made no outcry during the torture. Laubardemont was unable to extract the confession he needed. I refused to acknowledge myself guilty of magic, stating that I was no sorcerer and that the only crime I had committed was that of human frailty. I moaned and cried aloud greatly, and yet produced no tears, though was urged to weep often. Far from confessing to the charges of

177

witchery, I maintained my innocence and prayed prayers so earnest and true some of those present were moved to tears themselves.

(Grandier turns toward the painting of the Madonna and Child on the wall. He searches the Madonna's face, entreating it for some kind of answer, some sign of response, getting none. He looks down at his hands, draws a quick, shuddering breath.)

GRANDIER

It was a Friday … late afternoon. (*Speaking slowly, as though struggling to remember*) It had been a hot day … much like today. I was hoisted onto a cart drawn by six mules and paraded through the town. Loudun was filled to overflowing, thousands of people in every space, every window, on roofs and amongst the gargoyles of the churches, great multitudes, shouting and shoving, climbing up on every vantage point to get a glimpse of me. My hope was in God throughout. I prayed to Him continually, and even when I was lifted onto the layers of firewood, I continued saying litanies to the Blessed Virgin. The captain of the guard promised me that before the fire was lit, he would save me the pain of the fire and strangle me with a noose. I was tied to the stake and given the kiss of peace and told to brace myself for the end. It was then that I realized the final indignity that had been prepared for me.

(Grandier stares at Tom, a strange anger and fear in his eyes.)

TOM

What was it?

GRANDIER

My funeral pyre was facing the house of the king's
prosecutor in Loudun; a Monsieur Louis Trincant, my
staunchest and most resolute enemy. He sat at the
window of his drawing room, laughing triumphantly
whilst raising a glass in salute to me. The spectacle of
his triumph moved me to shame and bitterness, and I
lowered my eyes, lest I say something I regret. In the
same moment I noticed a thin blue vapor of smoke
rising from beneath me – the pyre had been lit! The
smoke turned into a crackling flame, and it was then
that I knew I had not been saved the pain of the fire by
strangulation.

*(Grandier refills the glass and drinks quickly, as though
trying to extinguish the memory of the flames. His voice
trembles. He has difficulty continuing.)*

GRANDIER

And then … then I did something.

TOM

What?

GRANDIER

I … oh … my son –*(He crosses himself.)* Please forgive
me. Be my confessor. I want to tell you what I did.

TOM

Do so. Be calm.

GRANDIER

179

It was then that I cursed God!

(Grandier breaks off, terrified by the words he has just uttered. Two tears rolled from his eyes as he casts a frightened glance at the painting of the Madonna and Child. He closes his eyes so that he cannot see the icon. He recovers somewhat from the weeping, opens his eyes.)

GRANDIER

I *cursed* my Savior! I shouted out in protest! I wailed and screamed! I said that there was no God, no Christ, nothing but fear and loathing. I cast my eyes to heaven and mocked the saints. Before long, I was surrounded by a wall of flame, a curtain of black smoke. I screamed one last time *–to hell with God!*

(Grandier flinches. His voice grows cracked and hoarse, and his eyes glisten with the tears.)

GRANDIER

Almost to the instant of my curse, the fire of the Devil cut the rope to which I was tied to the stake, and I fell into the flames. And so, I died –the vilest and most despicable of God's servants.

(There is a long pause. Tom stares on, aghast. The tears are now crowding Grandier's eyes. Grandier takes a lace handkerchief from his pocket and dabs his nose.)

GRANDIER

Now you see why it is so urgent you attend to the indulgences. For my soul will languish forever in Purgatory if this sin is not blotted out from God's sight.

(There is another pause. Tom is about to say something. But before he can have a chance, Grandier rises from his chair.)

GRANDIER

I will not take up anymore of your time. Please remember to say the prayers for me.

TOM

But Father, I beg you stay.

GRANDIER

I must go. I am tired to death.

(Grandier takes his hat, empties his glass of wine, rolls up his cape under his arm, honors Tom with a bow, and exits to the right of the stage. The LIGHTS *of the stage dim to* BLACK-OUT.
The LIGHTS *come up on the public square. Tom is standing by the church, looking at his wristwatch. The chimes of the church tower strike seven o' clock, and then, from the left of stage, appears Grandier, carrying as before a laurel branch. He bows to Tom, detaching his hat, his cloak sweeping the floor.)*

GRANDIER

Good sir. I am delighted to be in your presence once again.

TOM

The same.

GRANDIER

I must apologize for being late. I offer you my excuses.

TOM

I am sure they are adequate.

GRANDIER

Your humble servant. I am afraid I was caught up with a little matter to do with my incarceration, a pressing engagement with a lawyer in Hades who is working on my case, a Dr Gottfried Leibniz, you may have heard of him.

TOM

Certainly.

GRANDIER

Wonderful man, very pleasant, for a German. Though I must confess I always hated the Teutonic tongue, but then I am prejudiced. God grant all is well with you?

TOM

Everything is okay.

(Grandier gives a bemused look.)

GRANDIER

Okay! What is this– ok *–ay*. I have heard it several times from you. Where does it derive?

TOM

It's American, I think.

GRANDIER

Ah! The New World! I always regret I never visited
there. Now, you could say, I have other pressing
matters. So, pray tell. Have you asked the council of
Jesus Christ?

TOM

In a sense.

GRANDIER

How do you mean?

TOM

The offering of silver and tolling of the church bells
were simple in themselves, but the prayers were more
difficult. I'm afraid I haven't darkened the door of a
church since I was a child. The sacramental act was
awkward, like witnessing a dead ceremony, full of dead
people. If you pardon the expression.

GRANDIER

That is ok –ay.

(They both laugh.)

TOM

Would you care for a walk, Reverend Father?

GRANDIER

I have no objection to a stroll on a sunny evening.

(The LIGHTS *on the area of stage dim to* BLACK-
OUT *and come up on the right-hand part of the stage
that is made to look like a small walled garden.*

Grandier and Tom enter from a gate on the left and sit down on a bench. The lengthening shadows of the evening are visible. Grandier looks around the garden, a smile on his lips.)

GRANDIER

This is a very happy garden. It wasn't here when I was alive. If I recall, there was a stable, with a blacksmiths attached.

TOM

Yes, it is very pleasant.

GRANDIER

A refuge of happy consolations.

TOM

Do you miss your own age?

GRANDIER

It was a vale of wretchedness my child –a fools' paradise!

TOM

Your accusers sounded unscrupulous.

GRANDIER

They wanted nothing else but my blood! Ah-h! *(rasps bitterly)* –What swine's they were! I can still see their hated faces, faces where all joy, hope, health, tenderness, and warmth were stripped from. Such vulgar folk! Hypocrites to the last, more experienced in wrangling than all the clerks of Paris. To think the same people who praised my actions and kissed my feet were

184

in the next instant rushing forward to heap up the embers on my fire *(He clicks his tongue against his teeth.),* Tch –ch.

TOM

And they got what they wanted –your confession.

GRANDIER

I am sure my curse of God was interpreted as such.

(There is a pause. Tom looks down at the ground with a puzzled frown.)

GRANDIER

Is there something which bothers you?

TOM

Yes, of sorts.

GRANDIER

Then say it.

TOM

You have given your reasons for being in Purgatory, and even though I find them difficult to accept, I must believe what you tell me. But something else confuses me. Forgive me for my Calvinistic impertinence, but why do you think you were condemned by God for such an utterance?

GRANDIER

Just as something is worthy of the greatest reward when it is done properly, so it is deserving of the severest punishment by the gravest offence.

TOM

I would hardly say cursing God is the gravest offence, especially if done in such a dreadful situation.

(*Grandier removes his wide-brimmed hat and scratches his head, looks around the garden, staring at the quickening shadows.*)

GRANDIER

Ever since I was a child, I have longed for a place like this; an enclosed oasis of rest, a place where I can live complete, as complete as Adam when he came from the hands of God.

(*Grandier strokes his Van Dyke beard. His eyes are distant.*)

GRANDIER

My childhood was exceptional. I was preternaturally bright and precocious, full of eager learning and moral integrity. I had a gift for languages and oratory and became a perfect master of Greek, second to Latin, and then Hebrew, on account of the holy scriptures, also of Chaldean and Arabic, for the same reason. I had great religious fervour and received my education at the Jesuit College of Bordeaux. There, I was a brilliant pupil. The Jesuits from a young age had me targeted for greatness. Indeed, I would have made a good classics scholar if I were not presented to the important living of St Peter's Church in Loudun, along with priest and canon of the collegial church of the Holy Cross, a position with a substantial annual income and considerable prestige.

(Grandier smiles, a trifle grimly.)

GRANDIER

I dined with the most learned men of my age. I held
company with poets, painters, composers, philosophers,
radical thinkers, the cultural elite of France. My
erudition and wit made me a favorite visitor to the great
houses of Loudun. People flocked to my church to hear
my sermons. I was handsome, charismatic, eloquent, a
man of power and influence, of sound doctrine and
secular learning. I developed my own doctrine, writing
a treatise questioning the celibacy of the priesthood,
doubting such things as the Incarnation … the Divinity
of Christ … the Resurrection … Virgin birth …
Transubstantiation … undermining the most basic
doctrines of the Church. I acknowledged that I had no
faculty for setting such theological questions; that I had
an earthly mind and that I would devote no more time
to solving problems that were not of this world. I still
gave sermons on salvation, but my heart was far from
God. I praised Christ on my lips, but gave credence to
the Greek sages that maintained that life is the
beginning and end of all things, that some unearthly
existence did not count –that I was destined to die a
death which I shall never return.

*(Grandier pauses for a moment, considering the irony
of what he has said.)*

GRANDIER

I became a man of the world, a sensualist and pleasure-
seeker. I thought everything of the body and nothing of
the soul. I indulged myself on whatever I pleased: wine
–whores –dice. In words and forms I was still a

187

Christian. In thoughts and acts and feelings, I had never worshipped anything but myself – *My* kingdom come. *My* will be done –the kingdom of lust and greed and vanity, the will to cut a figure, the will to trample underfoot, to triumph and exult.

(Grandier forces his lips into a smile, but his eyes remain distant.)

GRANDIER

One night, not long after the accusations of devilry against me, a great weight began to press down upon me. The house I lived in became too constricted. I felt suffocated and so went quietly downstairs, slipped into the yard, opened the street door, and dashed out into the night. The moon was about to set; its light had already waned. There wasn't a sound. All the lamps were out; the city was asleep in God's bosom. I spread my arms and took a long breath and prayed in earnest to God. I knew I was a weak, bad man … that I was a lover of the world … that I had lived by the works of the flesh. I had silk clothes and red feathers in my hats and gold rings, gifts leant to me by Satan – well, I wanted to give them all back! I cried aloud in the streets … tore my clothes … ground my teeth … flung myself on the earth, weeping. At that moment a thought came to me, an idea seized sovereignty in my mind. I experienced a vivid sense of liberty, of understanding. I realised that I hated the world … that I hated people … and most of all … more than anything else … more than all the power … riches … women … *I hated myself.* For the first time I understood the meaning of contrition –not doctrinally, not by scholastic definition, but from within, as an anguish of regret and self-condemnation. It was as if I had been living my whole life in some sort

188

of unreality, some grey area of indifference, much like where I inhabit now. It didn't seem to torment me –this unreality. I accepted it fully … the sunlight … the food … the girls bodies … the trials and melancholy. Only through the recognition of my own mortality was I able to see my state more clearly. Only through the prospect of my own death was I able to take on a more mature understanding of my earthly existence. After that I knew what I must do.

TOM

You willed your own execution.

(Grandier looks Tom in the eye.)

GRANDIER

That is so. My trial would be my confession, my torture the affliction I must undertake for my faults and shortcomings, my death the penance by which I would atone for the sins of a vain and disordered life. I wept bitterly that night in the streets, not for what I was to suffer but for what I had become. The only thing I was afraid of was that I would lose heart during my tribulation.

TOM

Which you did.

(Grandier lowers his head.)

GRANDIER

I was weak … not strong enough … too feeble to bear the sufferings which God had been pleased to burden me.

TOM

And so all was lost.

GRANDIER

It was … long ago.

(*Grandier hides his face in his hands. After a moment, Tom puts his hand on his shoulder; the priest does not move, sunk in that lost world, buried in that incommunicable and tongueless past.*)

GRANDIER

So long ago.

(*After another pause, Tom lowers his hand from Grandier's shoulder and sits with him in an attitude of quiet reverie.*)

TOM

What is man that thou art mindful of him?

(*Tom suddenly sits up, stands, kneels before Grandier, takes his hand and kisses it. Grandier looks at him in surprise.*)

TOM

Reverend, sir. I have an idea.

GRANDIER

What is it?

TOM

Maybe you have already been forgiven for your sins. Maybe you have been keeping yourself in this strange imprisonment by your own volition.

(Grandier looks at Tom, his confusion turning to intrigue.)

TOM

My suspicion is that Purgatory doesn't exist. It is just a human condition, not based on God's word in scripture. Like every Christian before or since, you have felt you have a responsibility to your eternal soul. To freely reject the grace offered by God is the gravest sin. But you had not rejected God's grace. You accepted your wrongs. You have asked God to forgive you for your atheism and idolatry. You have asked God to forgive you for your moment of weakness at the stake – is that not enough?

(Grandier folds his hands in his lap, drops his eyes to the ground, his face a mask of thought.)

TOM

Perhaps all these years you have *felt* you have sinned against God, that you have locked yourself out of heaven, when all the while you have been living within the conscious love of God. Perhaps the question is not how you or anybody should prepare themselves for heaven, but how is God to redeem and renew his creation *through his creation.*

(Grandier strokes his Van Dyke beard)

GRANDIER

You think so? Hm.

TOM

Were we not made to live on earth?

GRANDIER

We were.

TOM

And is not the flesh to be reconciled with the spirit?

GRANDIER

It is.

TOM

Then perhaps you are already where you should be, perhaps the supernatural age is already here – that you are already *resurrected.*

(*Grandier continues stroking his Van Dyke beard in an impressed manner. He stares into the twilight of the garden. A tear threatens to escape his eyes. Instead, he rises. A man can be seen standing at the garden gate, tall and dark, bearded, wearing a tunic as white as snow, with a purple mantle over his shoulder. A fresh green holly branch laden with gleaming berries crowns his long hair. Grandier moves towards the man. He halts, and for a minute stands with the man at the gate. He looks back at Tom, his lips move, but nothing comes out. When he walks on, it is in a jovial mood.*)

There is silence. The LIGHTS *dim to* BLACK-OUT *as*

the CURTAIN *falls*

non est priorum memoria sed nec eorum quidem
quae postea futura sunt erit recordatio apud eos
qui futuri sunt in novissimo
Ecclesiastes 1:11

Lightning Source UK Ltd.
Milton Keynes UK
UKHW010644091020
371302UK00001B/185